THE ZERO HOUR

BY BEN GRAZIOSE

Copyright © 2012 by Ben Graziose
First Edition – June 2012

ISBN
978-1-77097-481-4 (Hardcover)
978-1-77097-482-1 (Paperback)
978-1-77097-483-8 (eBook)

All rights reserved.

No part of this publication may be reproduced in any form, or by any means, electronic or mechanical, including photocopying, recording, or any information browsing, storage, or retrieval system, without permission in writing from the publisher.

This book is a work of fiction. Names, characters, places, and incidents either are the product of the author's imagination or are used fictitiously, and any resemblance to actual persons, living or dead, business establishments, events, or locales is entirely coincidental.

Published by:

FriesenPress
Suite 300 – 852 Fort Street
Victoria, BC, Canada V8W 1H8

www.friesenpress.com

Distributed to the trade by The Ingram Book Company

For my family

Kari, Amanda and Megan

*Thank you for all your love, unrelenting support
and encouragement throughout this project.*

Sage Breslin, Alyson Fitzgerald and Lauren Calderon

For pushing this project over the finish line.

Table of Contents

Chapter 1	1
Chapter 2	7
Chapter 3	11
Chapter 4	17
Chapter 5	21
Chapter 6	27
Chapter 7	37
Chapter 8	43
Chapter 9	53
Chapter 10	57
Chapter 11	65
Chapter 12	71
Chapter 13	79
Chapter 14	89
Chapter 15	95
Chapter 16	103
Chapter 17	109
Chapter 18	119
Chapter 19	125
Chapter 20	133
Chapter 21	145
Chapter 22	151
Chapter 23	157
Chapter 24	161
Chapter 25	169
Chapter 26: Epilogue	173

Chapter 1

Tony Evans got out of his car on his way to work as he had every morning for the better part of 30 years. He looked up for a moment, taking in the sun on his face. The air was cool and crisp this October morning, even though the morning fog had ignored most of San Francisco. Tony reached into his car and pulled out his well-worn backpack, faded and beaten over the years, much like Tony. Closing the car door, Tony stared at his reflection in the driver's side window, studying his weathered face and fading hair. Though Tony was only 51, he appeared older. As his reflection stared back at him, he noticed the lines creeping around his eyes and the gray hair that had slowly taken over his natural brown color, seemingly overnight. Tony's hair was thinning on top but not to the point where he felt he had to wear hats or shave his head, at least not yet. He knew that that day would be coming soon though.

Sighing deeply and filled with a sense of dread, Tony turned and started his walk across the parking lot and into the San Francisco Chronicle, the predominate newspaper servicing the San Francisco area since 1865, when it was founded by Charles and Michael deYoung. The Chronicle had been an institution in the Bay Area since its inception, delivering the news on a daily basis to San Francisco's 7 million people. As popular as the Chronicle had been to the Bay area's population, evolving technology had led to the decline of print media. Long gone were the days of people leisurely reading the newspaper while drinking coffee in diners and cafés, on the subway, or in the kitchen. The process had been replaced by the quick upload of electronic data delivered to every computer, cell phone or tablet for instant consumption. All that failed to evolve was left behind. Today Tony realized that he was one of those being left behind.

Tony entered the busy news room witnessing the daily chaos as people ran back and forth with printouts in one hand and coffee in the other. He walked to his desk and tossed his backpack on to his chair which promptly dropped to the floor. Tony just stared at it and slowly took off his jacket and flipped it over the back of his old brown chair that squeaked and wobbled every time it was used. Tony slumped in his chair, and turned on his computer screen. The electronic glow stared back at him and he hunted and pecked his username and password on the key board with his two index fingers. For a newspaper man, Tony could type fast, but no one would accuse him of typing correctly. He'd always been a two finger typist, and nothing in this world would change that.

Tony leaned back in his chair and looked around the news room. The large area with rows and rows of cubicles was filled with people typing stories or making phone calls to confirm story facts. There was a charge in the air today, but not of the news variety. It had been known for quite some time that change was coming to the paper. Speculations about the nature of this change had been the topic of water cooler conferences and rumor for the better part of a year. Anyone working at the paper knew that circulation, readership, and advertising revenue was down. Web traffic for the electronic version of the paper was up, and it was just a matter of time before there would be a shift in staffing—just what the shift would entail was the black cloud hanging over the pressroom.

"Hey, Tone! You in that meeting in 10 minutes?" said Bobby Jenkins, a young twenty something up-and-coming sports reporter.

Bobby always dressed in the latest fashion and had the inside scoop on every aspect of local baseball, football, basketball and hockey. Even though Bobby was young, he came to the paper right out of Stanford's journalism program and became an instant hit. His easy demeanor and strong writing skills resulted in a solid, yet small readership.

"Yeah. You heading over there now?" Tony said, dejectedly.

"No, I'm on my way out to a press conference this morning down at the 'Niners facility." Bobby said as he passed Tony's cubicle.

"Catch ya later, man."

"See ya, Bobby."

Tony followed a large group of older reporters and assistants into the main conference room. The large meeting room was furnished with a long dark oak stained conference table and large leather seats with additional chairs brought in from nearby cubicles. Overhead florescent lighting gave the room a soft glow. The staff gathered around the chairs and started to take their seats. It wasn't lost on the people in the room that the average age of everyone present was north of fifty. Those without seats lined the walls.

Carol Gibson, the Chronicle's Editor-in-Chief walked confidently into the room. Her blonde hair was pulled back in a ponytail. When Carol's hair was in a ponytail everyone knew that something serious was going down. Carol was in her mid-to-late thirties, and her demeanor demanded attention. She was followed into the room by a very young assistant from human resources, whose arms were laden with large manila envelopes with hand-written names on the front. The young assistant moved through the room, handing out the envelopes, and the room settled down to a quiet hum as Carol moved to the front of the conference table to address the staff.

"Ladies and Gentlemen, you may have heard the rumors by now, and if you're in this room, then you know they're true. The paper has taken massive hits over the years, and readership is way down. The print era is on the decline and the paper can no longer keep staff at its current levels. As of this morning, the paper has made the decision to eliminate all your positions effective immediately. HR is passing around your separation packets."

Tony's heart sunk. As he looked around the room at his colleagues' empty eyes, the reality of the situation hit home. Everyone knew this was a long time coming. It had been water cooler talk for months. But until Tony heard the fatal words, "your position has been eliminated," it was just that, talk. It wasn't real. Not until today. Everyone deals with losing their livelihood in different ways. Meredith Adams, 62 years old, assistant and grandmother of 5 sobbed into her hands and were comforted by her friends. Bart Johnson, 55 years old and a fact checker, exploded into a tirade of cursing under his breath wondering what he was going to do now. He lived a lonely existence, and coming to work was all he had to look forward to in an otherwise sad and devoid life. Now that his job was gone, he would only fall deeper into his hidden depression. Randy Smith, 48 years old and a photographer, on the other hand was elated. Tony stared at him intently as Randy was all smiles. He had been telling everyone that he was riding it out until the end to pick up any severance the paper will give him and going into the photo business with his younger brother. This was the start of his new life, and he looked forward to it whole-heartedly. Tony continued to scan the room, one by one, and noticed there was more sadness than elation like Randy's. Tony's thoughts soon turned to himself and what exactly he was going to do next. He was

51 and being a newspaper man was pretty much all he knew. It was everything to him. It defined him and consumed him. The price he paid to the paper was very large. Tony had been loyal and dedicated throughout the years, and now it was over. In one swift action of an executive's pen, the very thing that defined Tony had been taken away. Tony was running the gauntlet of emotions but the one that sat with him the most was emptiness. Now what? Carol continued her instructions and as her assistant handed him his exit package in a plain non-descript envelope; Tony didn't really hear anything more. He was just going through the motions. Noise filled his ears as he stared blankly at his envelope.

The worst part was yet to come. Carol completed her instructions and left the meeting. One by one the former employees of the San Francisco Chronicle signed their paperwork, received their final checks and exited back to their desks to clear out their personal belongings. As Tony made his way back to his desk, he could not help noticing the eyes of those around him staring at him. He arrived at his desk to find boxes had already been delivered to his workstation, waiting to be packed with his personal effects. People slowly shuffled up to Tony to say their goodbyes. Some hugged him, even people he was not very close with. Some shook his hand. Some just didn't know what to say. Tony nodded politely and completed his task. With one last, long look at his former working space, Tony tossed is backpack over his shoulder, threw his coat over the boxes, took the stack of boxes into his arms, and started his last walk down the corridor to the parking lot. Not knowing why, Tony felt a sense of guilt like he had done something to warrant his release from the paper. Most of all, Tony felt the anxiety and the need to just get out of there. He was not comfortable being part of the spectacle that was going on. Tony turned his hip into the door and silently exited, welcoming the slamming of the door behind him and allowing the sound to echo in his ears.

Chapter 2

A few hours later, Tony entered his apartment, carrying the large boxes of his office belongings, with his backpack slung over his shoulder. He kicked the door closed with his foot and moved to the kitchen table where he dropped the large boxes with a thud. The apartment was sparsely decorated. Pictures had been removed from the walls, leaving their outlines scattered on the dirty walls. Empty boxes littered the hallway along with tattered blankets, old photo albums, and other discarded items. Dishes filled the sink, and food and coffee stained the tile of the kitchen counters. Tony sat at his dining room table, gazing at the chaos of his apartment, realizing that his soon-to-be ex-wife and daughter took pretty much everything when they moved out.

Amy and Tony met thirteen years ago in New York when Tony was on vacation there. One Saturday night, Tony and his friends were downing "Irish Car Bombs" in Connolly's when Amy walked in with a group of girls. The moment Tony saw Amy; he was attracted to her and made his way across the bar to talk to her. After an hour of conversation, he was hooked. He couldn't take his eyes off her long dark brown hair as it curled over her shoulders and across her breasts. Her black high heels accented her long and shapely legs. The low-cut red dress sealed the deal for Tony. They talked and drank all night, ignoring their friends and everyone around them. All they saw was one another, and that was all that mattered.

The instant attraction grew into something much more over the months of phone calls and emails. Tony struggled with email, but he was determined to understand just enough about America Online to get Amy's messages. Amy finished her last year at the Art Institute of New York and moved west to San Francisco to be closer to Tony. Amy loved the city and Tony. Before their first year of dating had ended, they moved in together. Before their second year together was up, Nicole was born. Tony couldn't have been happier. His work was going well. He was covering some of the biggest murder stories the city had to offer and was often featured on the front page. Amy worked part time in a local art shop and took care of little Nicki. One of Nicki's favorite spots was the flower gardens in Golden Gate Park. She would waddle around for hours, enthralled with the colorful foliage. The yellows, oranges, greens, and purples were mesmerizing to her. It was a place that would always make her smile. The years went by, and Tony and Amy grew apart. Tony was always chasing the next story, the next deadline, and the next byline. The pressures of full-time parenting left Amy unfulfilled and resentful Tony's work and its impact on his availability as a father. When he was there, he was great with Nicki, but those times were few and far between. Despite many opportunities, Amy remained faithful to Tony, regardless of the growing distance between them. Eventually, Amy couldn't stand it any longer and told Tony that she wanted to move out with Nicki. Tony was crushed, but resigned. It took Tony a few weeks to adjust to the fact his wife was leaving him and to find the courage to tell his daughter. When Tony was ready to disclose the plans for divorce, it was to Golden Gate Park's flower gardens that he took Nicki to explain the best he could.

"Why, Dad? Why is Mom leaving us?" Nicki pleaded.

"She's not leaving us, Honey. She's leaving ME."

"Why? What did you do?"

"Sometimes people just grow apart, Nicki. I can't really explain it...."

"Well TRY!" she screamed.

Tony stirred from his memory, as his home phone rang. He got up to answer it, but the caller ID announced that it was his soon-to-be ex-wife. He listened to Amy's voice as she left a message on the machine.

"Tony, just to let you know, I finished moving our stuff out today. I left the keys on the kitchen table. By the way, I forgot to tell you yesterday, but some guy came by—a courier—and left a letter for you. It's on the table with the rest of your mail. Listen, I'm sorry it didn't work out. I really am. Nicole and I will be at my parents for a while till we find a new place. Please don't call. Just give us a few days."

While Amy sounded strong and confident, Tony heard the pain beneath her words.

After Amy hung up, he looked at the flashing light on his answering machine, reached down, and clicked DELETE. He looked across the table at the stack of mail. He flipped through it, stopping to stare at a letter with the Department of Corrections seal and a return address from San Quentin. Tony tore it open and began to read its contents. Tony got as far as the name of the inmate before he stopped reading: Reynaldo Ramirez.

"Ramirez? Ramirez?" Tony whispered to himself.

The name was somehow hauntingly familiar to Tony, but his memory failed to place it. He scanned the rest of the letter, which requested his presence at the prison at 10a.m. the next day.

Then it hit him: Reynaldo Ramirez, serial killer. Ramirez was serving a death sentence for a series of murders of those known and unknown to him. Tony remembered covering his trial. Ramirez was a massive man, standing over six-foot-four with muscled guns protruding from his arms. His long jet black hair always seemed to cover his face, but his piercing coal black eyes beamed out through the tangled mass. During the trial, Ramirez stared down the witnesses. His tattooed arms rested heavily on the table, cuffed with handcuffs that looked too small against his flesh. Ramirez had been in trouble since he was a kid and had been charged with battery and attempted murder, but he'd escaped prison so far. Seems that each time he looked good for a conviction, key witnesses seemed to recant somewhere along the way. The police tried to keep tabs on Ramirez, but he disappeared.

In the summer of 1988, Ramirez resurfaced in Oakland. During the investigation of a domestic disturbance, police discovered a grisly scene. Wall-to-wall blood splattered everywhere, with a body count of five: four women and one man. Ramirez, his leg apparently broken during the killing spree, was unable to flee the scene before police apprehended him. Tony covered the story for the Chronicle from the arraignment to the trial and sentencing. During the trial, Ramirez didn't say much. The prosecutor claimed that the murders were a drug and prostitution situation gone wrong. Though drugs were found at the scene, Ramirez had none on him, and had no history of drug use. Ramirez offered no explanation, and in the eyes of the court, it didn't much matter; with five people dead, Ramirez had to pay. Following the trial, Ramirez was moved to San Quentin's death row, awaiting his zero hour.

Flipping open his out-of-date cell phone, Tony called the prison. After what seemed like forever, a woman answered.

"Yes, hello—I'm calling in regards to a letter I received. What? Yeah, ahhh, lemme just look for that. The ID on the letter is CDCR#E37102. Yeah I'll hold. Yes, Hi. I'm calling about a letter I received from Warden Hoffmann, in regards to an inmate, Reynaldo Ramirez. Do I really need to come out there? Yes, I can be there by ten. Wait, one more question: Will I be paid for this interview?"

Chapter 3

Early morning traffic was unusually light. Tony made his way over the Bay Bridge east towards Oakland, then north on the 580 freeway through Albany and Richmond. As Tony crossed the Richmond San Rafael Bridge, his nerves started to eat at him. It had been twenty-three years since he'd seen Ramirez. But last night, no amount of booze could erase the images of Ramirez or the bloody scene of his last murder. Throughout the night, and now, during his drive to the prison, Tony was fixated on two questions: "What in the hell does the Warden want with him and what how does Ramirez play into all of this?"

Tony and about fifteen other visitors moved slowly through the security procedures to enter the prison. IDs were checked against paper work, metal detectors scanned for weapons and names were recorded on the visitor's log. Hurry up and wait. Finally Tony made his way through the throng of friends and loved ones and headed to a waiting area. The stark room reminded Tony of the DMV as random people stared at smartphones and laptops as they waited. The grey walls were adorned with outdated posters, magazines from years gone by sat unread in racks and women and their children awaited the chance to see husbands, boyfriends, and fathers. Tony noticed that there was not a newspaper in sight. Twenty minutes later, a large guard came to retrieve Tony from the intellectual void. Tony stared at the badge announcing that "SAMSON" was the man towering over him.

"Mr. Evans? Please come with me."

Tony stood up, slung his backpack over his shoulder, and followed Samson down the hall towards Warden Hoffmann's office.

Tony was escorted into a large office that overlooked one of the exercise yards. Men in orange jumpsuits lifted weights, played basketball, or stood idly on the blacktop. The office was impressive and reminded Tony of a politician's office. The Warden's large oak desk was covered in neat stacks of office folders, and his books shelves were jammed with volume after volume of law books and procedural manuals. A Persian rug and a number of framed snapshots of the Warden with various political figures gave the office the air of posterity. Warden Hoffmann greeted Tony with a warm smile and firm handshake.

"Mr. Evans? So nice that you could come out here on short notice and see us. That'll be all, Samson."

Samson exited and closed the door behind him.

"Can I get you anything? Coffee? Water?" Hoffmann asked.

"No. I'm fine, thank you."

"Please be seated then."

Warden Hoffmann gestured to the chairs in front of his desk and took the seat behind it. Hoffmann had been at the helm for about five years, was a well-respected man in the law enforcement communities, and had a number of high-ranking friends in Sacramento. Though in his sixties, Warden Hoffmann was in great physical shape, with a full head of silver hair, wire-rimmed glasses, and only a slightly expanding waistline.

"I'm sure you're wondering why you are here." Warden Hoffmann started, as he lay his glasses down on the massive desk.

"Your letter said you wanted me to interview Reynaldo Ramirez?"

"Correct. Well, actually, we'd like you to conduct a series of interviews with Ramirez. You do remember him, don't you?"

"Of course—I covered the trial for the Chronicle."

"Ramirez is a real piece of work. He's killed at least nine people, though he claims the number is higher. He was on the FBI's 10 most wanted before he was caught. He's been pretty quiet here for the last 4 years and has mostly kept to himself.

But don't fool yourself, Evans, not even for a moment. That man would just as soon kill you as look at you."

Warden Hoffmann stared hard at Tony.

"And how did I draw this assignment?"

"He asked for you."

"What? How? Why?"

"He asked for you by name."

"Who the hell am I to him?"

"I was going to ask the same thing Mr. Evans."

Tony stared at the warden, confused.

"His lawyer filed motions so that he could tell his story. He petitioned the court on a freedom of speech angle and by some grace of God won. Since he's set to exit this world in less than seven days, it's not worth the tax payer's money to appeal. So here you are. Do you have your gear with you?"

"Yeah I've got it with me. But, what if I'm not interested in hanging out with a serial killer for the next week? Especially one who's asked to see me personally? Truthfully, I'm not too comfortable with that." Tony confessed.

"Here's the court order." the warden said as he handed Evans a sheath of papers. "You don't have much of a choice Mr. Evans. If you need, you can give that to your work for the time off you'll need."

"That won't be a problem. You could consider me a freelance journalist at the moment."

"Well then, it's settled. Look at it as a 7 day contract. You're on your own to conduct the interviews, though we'll be reviewing everything your write before you go to press. Samson will show you the interview room we setup for you."

Warden Hoffmann summoned his assistant, stood up, and extended his hand to Tony.

"Samson will take you to the interview room and review our protocol with you. You are NOT to deviate from these rules in any way, shape, or form. Is that clear Mr. Evans?"

"Yes, Warden." Tony responded as he shook the warden's hand.

"Ramirez, locked up or not, is a dangerous man. I don't support this nonsense, but we must comply with the court order. He will be chained and in restraints at all times. Are there any questions?"

"No, sir—not that I can think of. Um… I can use my recorder, right?" Tony asked.

"Yes, that will be fine. Good luck, Mr. Evans."

Samson and Tony walked down a series of corridors leading away from the administration wing and towards the housing wing. The walls, floor, and ceiling were all painted in the same dull grey color with bright overhead fluorescent light. As they reached heavily armored doors, Samson's booming voice startled Tony out of his observational reverie.

"Do not approach the inmate at any time. Do not pass him any items at any time. Do not share personal information about yourself to him. Trust me—you don't want him in your head. You will have a small table in the room, and you will have one pen, notepaper, and your tape recorder, that's it. Every day on your way in and out, you will be inventoried for said items. Do not cross the yellow line on the floor at any time. The prisoner will be seated and chained at all times. We're here."

A loud buzzing echoed through the hall, followed by clicks which indicated the release of the door's security locks. Samson opened the door and allowed Tony to enter the room. The room's decor was the same dull grey, brightly lit with florescent light. There was a small metal table with a single uncomfortable-looking wooden chair in the center of the room. A large steel divider separated visitor and inmate. A metal chair for the inmate had been bolted to the floor on the other side of the divider. Tony moved to the table, opened his backpack, and removed his tape recorder. After closing up the pack, he handed it to Samson.

"I'll return this to you when you're done. Have a seat. We'll bring the inmate to you shortly. If you need any assistance or something goes wrong, hit this panic button. Knock on the door when you need to leave. A guard will be stationed outside at all times. We'll be monitoring you from the eye in the sky." noted Samson as he jerked his head towards the security camera in the corner of the ceiling.

"You have any questions?"

"Yeah—has anyone ever used that panic button?"

"Only once." Samson replied as he exits the room, closing the door firmly behind him, followed by the loud clang of the security bolt locking into place.

"Great." Tony took his coat off, placed it over the back of the chair and sat rigidly, staring at the chair soon to be filled by Renaldo Ramirez.

Chapter 4

After about fifteen minutes, the holding cell door opened and Reynaldo Ramirez shuffled into the cage, escorted by Samson and another guard. After twenty-three years, Ramirez was no less menacing. He had used his time to hone his two hundred and fifty pounds of muscle. His long black hair was now streaked with silver as it fell across his face. Ramirez's black piercing eyes locked onto Tony's as he shuffled to the metal chair.

Samson barked, "Sit your ass down, Ramirez."

Ramirez sank into the chair. The guards transferred the prisoner's restraints to the metal loops on the floor. Finished, the guards exited and bolted the door. Ramirez and Tony sat motionless, sizing each other up. Ramirez could sense Tony's anxiety. Tony was further disturbed by Ramirez's cold and confident demeanor.

"Mr. Evans." Ramirez began.

"Mr. Ramirez, why am I here?"

"Because I asked you to be."

"I'm here because the court required me to respond to the order, not because you asked me."

"Would you have come if I had?"

"No."

"Ha! Well there you go then, amigo".

"First off, I'm not your friend. And second, what the hell do you want from me?"

"I want you to tell my story".

"Your what?" Tony questioned.

"My story. That is what reporters do, right? I want you to write about me, and put me in the papers."

"Why on earth would I do something like that?" Tony asked, leaning back in his chair.

"Because you want to. You wanted to years ago, when you asked my lawyers for exclusive interviews during my trial. Because what you printed about me was fair and honest. I don't have much time left, and I want you to tell my story."

"You're crazy. You want me to tell your story now? No one even remembers you. I didn't remember you. I had to look it up. All that activist noise about saving you or killing you, not even front page news, man. You're just another murderer waiting to die. That's it, end of story. Not much more to tell." Tony said exasperated.

"That's where you're wrong, my friend. There IS a story. There WILL be a story, and you're going to write it." Ramirez said confidently.

"I am NOT your friend. And this is bullshit! I'm out of here." Tony retorted, grabbing the tape recorder off the table and reaching for his coat.

"SIT DOWN, MR. EVANS!" Ramirez yelled at Tony, never moving his eyes away from Tony's.

The guard at the door peered in the room through the bulletproof glass of the door, looking first at Tony, then at Ramirez, then disappearing to the side. Tony paused as his anger turned to fear. He placed his jacket back on the chair and sat, then placed his tape recorder back on the table, and turned it on. Tony looked back to Ramirez to meet his eyes.

"Maybe you don't understand what I am saying. I am not asking you to write my story. I am TELLING you to write this story." Ramirez said in a calm, cold, and calculated voice.

"And if I refuse?"

"Mr. Evans, if you refuse, then I will have to convince you. I'm pretty sure that you will not like that." Ramirez smiled through his long hair, exposing yellowed teeth.

"You're on Death Row. You're locked up. What can you possibly do to convince me to do this? And even if I wanted to, I can't."

"Yes, you can." Ramirez said growing impatient.

"No, I can't. You don't understand. I'm not a reporter anymore. I was laid off yesterday. I can't just waltz into the editor's office and demand they run this story." Tony pleaded.

"Well, that sounds like a personal problem. You better convince him."

"Even if I could, the story wouldn't run tomorrow. Maybe not even the next day—and no way it would run as a series."

"Mr. Evans, for a reporter you really disappoint me. What is all this 'I can't' bullshit?" Ramirez said in a deliberate tone. "You need to write this story like a life depends on it."

"Whose? Yours? Sorry, Ramirez, your nine lives are up on Sunday." Tony blurted out angrily.

The two men sat quietly, studying each other for a few minutes. The dead air hung heavily in the room.

"Tick Tock, Tony. Your time is running out."

"What did you mean, "You need to write this story like your life depends on it?"

"Not YOUR life—A life." responded Ramirez.

"Who's life?" Tony questioned nervously.

"Seems to me you're not getting this. You'll see—tonight. I think the 11 o'clock news will be your best bet."

"What the hell are you talking about?" Tony asked, now thoroughly confused.

Ramirez smiled at Tony.

"I'm going to offer you a little "incentive", if you will—to make sure you stay focused."

"Look—I don't understand what you're getting at! I need some time to think about it."

"You don't have much time, my friend. I'll tell you what: I'll see you tomorrow, first thing in the morning. We can discuss it then." Ramirez said confidently.

"I didn't say I'd do this, nor did I say I'd be back."

"You'll be back. My advice to you: watch the news. GUARD! "

The door opened up and Samson and his partner entered the room. They transferred the restraints from the bolts in the floor back to his shackles and moved him towards the door. Ramirez again maintained his gaze with Tony until the door was again shut. When the door was bolted, Tony reached out and turned off the tape recorder.

Tony leaned against his car outside the prison walls, breathing the air deep into his lungs. He pulled a cigarette out of his coat pocket, lit it, and took a long solid drag. He opened the door to his car, slid into the driver's side, and pulled his cell phone out of his pocket. He dialed the Chronicle's number, and punched in Carol Gibson's extension.

"Carol, it's Tony. I know I was laid off yesterday, but when you get this message, I need you to call me back as soon as possible. It's very important."

Chapter 5

That evening, Tony stepped out of a hot shower and toweled off, wiping the steam from the mirror in his bathroom. He threw on a t-shirt and shorts, grabbed a beer, and moved to the back of his sparse apartment. Unlatching the lock to the sliding glass door, he opened the door and walked out on the very small balcony. The balcony held two plastic chairs, a tiny plastic table. and the smallest Weber grill on the market. The table was grimy from months of sitting outdoors and was littered with empty beer cans and cigarette butts. Tony cleared a chair, opened a fresh pack of smokes, and sank into the chair. He took a deep swig of his beer and looked out over the dog park—which in truth is an empty lot between a liquor store and a coffee house.

As he watched the evening's dog walkers across the street, Tony chuckled. Here he is, living alone and still smoking outside. Amy hated his cigarette smoking, and for the most part, he only smoked on the job. She always complained about the odor on his clothes. Even though she'd moved out, he still felt like he had to sneak out for a quick smoke. He took the final drag off his cigarette, tossed the butt in an empty beer can, and headed back inside. As he walked past the kitchen, the clock on the microwave reminded him that it was nearing 11pm. Tony lay on his bed, reached for the remote control, flicked on the TV, and turned to the local news. Still shaken from his encounter with Ramirez earlier in the day, Tony found himself impatient with the commercials as he awaited the onset of newscast. As the 11 o'clock News logo appeared, Tony turned up the sound.

"Our top story tonight: an 11-year-old girl, identified as Nicole Evans, was abducted from her home in San Francisco earlier today. Police are asking for help from anyone who has any information on this case. An Amber Alert has been in effect since 6pm this evening. Again: Nicole Evans, 11-year-old, 4 feet, 9 inches, last seen wearing blue jeans and a white Justin Bieber T-shirt was abducted from her house late this afternoon. Please call the number on your screen if you have any information on the whereabouts of Nicole. Now let's go to Caroline Contaldo who is on the scene. Caroline, any update?"

Tony bolted upright in bed in horror and disbelief as he watched the scene unfolding live. Police cruisers and emergency vehicles were visible from aerial feed from the station's helicopter. Caroline Contaldo's report continued.

"I'm at the home where Nicole Evans and her mother have been staying. Word from our sources is that Nicole was taken sometime between 4 and 5 p.m. from her front yard. Police say they are investigating the abduction, and an Amber Alert is in effect for the missing girl. Police are asking for the public's help in getting Nicole home safely."

Tony grabbed his cell phone off the night stand next to the bed and called his soon-to-be ex-wife. She picked up on the third ring, in a hysterical voice.

"Tony!"

"Amy! My God, what happened? Are you alright? Nicki? What the hell is happening? I'm watching the news. What the hell is going on???"

"Tony! She's gone. Someone got my baby!" Amy screamed hysterically.

Fear gripped the air in Tony's lungs as panic spread through his body. Tony could hear Amy's cries on the other end of the phone but nothing was registering with him.

Tony squeezed every fiber of his being to speak, "I'm on my way."

Fifty torturous minutes later, Tony arrived at his in-laws' house. His in-laws had lived in the home overlooking Lake Merced for most of their adult lives. Tony's mind raced, unsure of what to expect on his arrival. News crews and police had crowded the street, forcing Tony to park down the street. The chaos around the house was insane; police officers and investigators canvassed the long driveway, front yard and porch. As Tony made his way towards the house, he was stopped by an SFPD officer.

The officer ordered Tony, "Sir, back away from the tape. This is a crime scene."

"No! Let me by! This is my in-laws' place! It's my daughter who's missing!" Tony demanded.

"Who are you?"

"Tony Evans, my daughter, Nicki is the missing girl! That is my in-law's place, my wife Amy is in there!" Tony forced out sounding desperate.

"Mr. Evans! Please come with me, sir!"

The officer led Tony through the doorway and seated him in the living room, surrounded by a dozen or so members of the investigative team. Tony looked around the normally meticulous room at the disorder left by the efforts of the crime scene team and shook his head. His mother-in-law would lose it when she saw what they'd done to her home. He stood for a moment taking this all in, then headed upstairs to his in-laws' bedroom. He was met by two SFPD officers flanking his mother-in-law, Lindsay. Upon seeing Tony, Lindsay sprang from the bed where she'd been sitting and hugged Tony warmly.

"Tony! I'm so glad you're here! I can't believe this is happening!" Lindsay cried.

"Lindsay, where's Amy?"

"She's in her room—she's just beside herself."

"I need to see her."

"Yes, yes, of course."

Tony made his way down the hall to Amy's room. The door was open and like Lindsay, Amy was surrounded by SFPD officers. The room was painted in a soft cream color with dark read trim. Like the downstairs living room, the room once had everything in its place but now was in a violent state of disarray. Amy stood at the window, stared down at the police activity below, clutched a Kleenex and Nicki's favorite teddy bear, and wept. Tony's heart broke when he saw Amy. It took three tries before Tony could get her name out of his mouth.

"Amy."

"Tony! Oh, God! Tony!" Amy broke her trance and threw herself into Tony's arms.

"Amy, what happened?"

An FBI Agent, dressed in a blue suit with matching tie approached Amy and Tony. He was a tall, muscular black man, with small-rimmed glasses, a shaved head, and a graying goatee. His FBI badge hung around his neck, and his demeanor was all business as he interrupted their conversation.

"Excuse me, who are you?" the FBI Agent asked Tony.

"I'm Tony Evans—Amy's husband and Nicki's father."

"I'm Lorenzo Callcut, FBI. I'm heading up the investigation in conjunction with SFPD. I'll need to ask you some questions."

"Of course. Can you give me a few minutes?" Tony asked, holding Amy close.

"Make it short—we're losing time. Clear the room." Callcut instructed the other officers. After the police left the room, Amy sat on the end of the bed, as Tony grabbed a chair and pulled it over to face Amy.

"Amy, what happened?" Tony asked softly.

"I picked up Nicki from school just like I always do. Nicki wanted to make cupcakes tonight, so we grabbed some stuff from the store. We got back and she helped me unpack the car, then went to her room to do her homework. Afterwards she was playing outside with some of the neighborhood kids." Tears slid down her face as Amy replayed the story for what seemed like the millionth time that day.

"It was getting dark, so I called for her to come inside, but there was no one out in the yard. I went out, looked up and down the street but didn't see her. I called her cell with no answer. I found Tommy, the boy next door. He and his sister play with Nicki all the time. He said that Nicki had told them she had to go home an hour ago, and that was the last time they saw her."

"What do you mean 'had to go home?'" Tony asked.

"He said she got a text to come home. So she left and came back home. But I didn't text her to come home." Amy said.

"What time was all this?"

"I'm, I'm not sure. Around dusk, so what? About 6:30 or so tonight."

"That's when you noticed her gone?"

"Yeah, I called all her friends in the neighborhood. Then Dad called the police. Why?" Amy asked, concerned.

"When did she go out to play? When did you get home?" Tony asked desperately.

"Ahhh—around 4:30-4:45 I guess."

"Damn!" Tony said, realizing that she was taken after Tony met with Ramirez.

"What? What is it Tony? What are you not telling me?" Amy demanded searching deep into Tony's eyes.

"No, no—it's nothing. I'm just trying to piece the timeline together, that's all. What was she wearing?" Tony asked.

"She was wearing a t-shirt with the picture of that singer that she likes, that kid, Justin something-or-other and blue jeans. And she was wearing the necklace we gave her for Christmas last year. She always wears that." Amy added.

"Did you see anyone? Anyone odd or unfamiliar? Did anyone come to the house—newspaper guys? Salesmen? Anyone?"

"No, no one like that. What are you getting at? What are you not telling me, Tony?" Amy asked suspiciously.

"It's nothing, really, Amy. I'm just trying to work this out. It'll be fine. Nicki's going to be fine! Nothing will happen to her, I swear it!"

Chapter 6

First thing in the morning, Tony made his way to the prison to see Ramirez again, just as Ramirez had demanded. As Tony made his way through the morning commute traffic, he replayed his memories of the night before. After meeting with Amy and calming her down, he met with Agent Callcut. Though Callcut didn't openly accuse Tony, it was obvious that Callcut suspected him of the kidnapping. After years of covering missing persons' cases for the Chronicle, Tony knew that the non-custodial parent was always at the top of the list when it came to abductions. He prayed that Callcut would come to his senses and discover evidence to assist in the recovery of his daughter.

Tony entered the interview room and tossed his backpack down on the table once again. He removed his recorder and returned the backpack to the guard. Ramirez was already in his seat, chains in place. Ramirez sat intently, staring at Tony through his long black and silver hair.

"What the hell have you done? Are you insane? Tell me you had nothing to do with my kid being taken!" Tony screamed at Ramirez, unable to contain himself any longer.

Tony paced back and forth, his anger growing by the moment as he yelled at the chained killer.

"Settle down, Tony. Sit." Ramirez said coldly.

"Fuck you! I..."

"Sit down. If you want answers, you'll sit your ass down."

Tony moved around the table and sat in the chair, facing Ramirez.

"So, now, do you want to tell me what you're ranting about?" Ramirez continued in his cold calculated tone.

"My daughter! Where did you take my daughter? I want her back right now!" Tony screamed.

"I'm glad I was able to get your attention. So, do we understand each other now?"

"Who do you have working for you? Don't you hurt her! She's got nothing to do with any of this! Where is she?" Tony demanded.

"That is not your concern at the moment. You have to stay focused. You have stories to write and publish. If you pay attention, then you just maybe able to save that girl."

"That GIRL, you ASSHOLE, is my daughter!" Tony yelled.

Ramirez smiled through his hair at Tony, but didn't react to Tony's anger.

"Why the hell are you doing this to me?" Tony continued desperately.

"You're asking the wrong questions. You've got five days till my zero hour to get my story heard and to save that kid."

"So, she's still alive?"

"That's all up to you. For now, yes. When I meet the zero hour, so will she. That is, if you can find her. And if you even think about going to the cops, I will say nothing more, and she will die. Her location dies with me on Sunday at midnight. If I find out that cops are involved, I'll have her killed and you'll never find her ragged little body. So, are you going to save this girl, hero?"

"You bastard." Tony said, tears streaming down his face.

"That's true, I am, but you didn't answer the question. When I die, that's on the state. When she dies, that's on you. You will have to live with that for the rest of your life. You'll have to look in the mirror and into your dead eyes and live with knowing you could have saved her, but you bitched out and did nothing. And because of that she'll be dead."

"God Damnit! Fine, I'll do it. She isn't going to die. I'll do this bullshit you want me to do. And I can't wait till you're dead."

"You may rethink that by Saturday night. You have your recorder?"

"Yes." Tony reached into his backpack and pulled out the tape recorder and clicked "Record."

"Good, let's get started."

Tony sat in the darkened booth of Harry's Tavern. Harry's was a local hang-out for reporters since it was two blocks away from the Chronicle. The place had a great friendly atmosphere and a variety of beer on tap. Known for their lunch and happy hour specials, the bar was hopping most afternoons and well into the night.

Tony ordered a Seven and Seven and found his way to the back of the bar to be alone with his thoughts. The bartender, a pretty blonde named Sally, brought him his drink. She smiled warmly at Tony and put his drink down, then returned to her business behind the bar. Tony sipped his drink as Bobby Jenkins slid into the seat across from him.

"Tone, isn't it a little early to be hitting that? Sorry to hear about you and the others being laid off yesterday. That really sucks, man. I was kinda surprised to get your message. I'm here—what is the big emergency?" Bobby asked.

"My daughter..."

"Your daughter? What about her?"

"She was taken last night. She's been kidnapped."

"Wait—what? She was taken last night? What the hell? Are you serious? My God, man, I'm sorry! What'd the cops say?" Bobby asked.

"Nothing. They don't know anything. And I can't go to them. If I do, she's dead."

"What? What are you talking about?"

"I know who took her—or at least the guy who's responsible for this shit. He's in San Quentin. He's giving me a chance to save her if I do him a favor. I've got till Sunday midnight to get it done, or she dies." Tony said somberly.

"Holy shit! Anything I can do?"

"He wants me to write about him. That's where you come in: I need you to do it for me. I want you to write a daily series, starting now and running through Saturday." Tony said staring at Bobby.

"Wait, Tony—a series? Just like that? I don't know if Carol will go for that. Maybe we can spin it like an exclusive? She may go for that, but she already has me on assignments. Sports stuff is really my game, man—how do you expect me to do this right?"

Tony looked around the semi-empty room, making sure no one was watching.

"You've GOT to do this, Bobby! Nicki will die if I don't get that story in the paper. I called Carol last night, but she didn't believe me either. The guy behind this is Ramirez: Reynaldo Ramirez. You remember that sick bastard?"

"Yeah, he had what nine, ten bodies to his credit? He's scheduled to opt out on Sunday."

"It's him. He's behind this. This is all some insane game to him. He gets one more if she dies, or I save her and he gets his name in the paper again. I have no choice! I NEED your help on this. It has to be my by-line."

"What? I'm writing for you? I don't even get credit for the pieces?"

"Look—I need you to do this! You can run an exclusive about how he blackmailed me on Sunday—and get credit for the series AND the exclusive—once he's dead. I can't look for her and write at the same time. That's what he wants: to set me up so I can't find her in time. He wants me to feel like he does: watching every second pass and know that time is running out. He's screwing with me." Tony said, squeezing Bobby's arm in desperation.

"Excuse me, gentlemen. Is one of you Tony Evans?" Sally asked, holding a large envelope in her hands.

"That's me." Tony replied.

"Here you go. That man at the bar asked me to give this to you." Sally turned and pointed towards the bar, then lowered her arm, realizing that the barstool was now empty.

"That's odd. He was just here." Sally said, confused.

Tony opened the envelope and pulled out a photograph. Tearing up, he held out a photo to Bobby. Nicole, face stained with tears, was tied to a chair and had duct tape over her mouth. Taped to her chest was a piece of paper showing today's date. Bobby dropped the photo like it was on fire and looked up at Tony.

"Oh my God! Tony, I'm in! I'll do whatever you need. I'll go back to the office and convince Carol right now. Now, what am I supposed to write again?" Bobby asked.

Tony pulled his tape recorder out of his backpack, ejected the tape, and handed it over to Bobby.

"I'm supposed to meet him every morning at 7:00 a.m. to get the "story" for the day. Everything you need is on the tape. You gotta get a front page story in print every day. I don't know if anything else will satisfy him." Tony added.

"What about the cops?" Bobby asked.

"Ramirez said no cops. He said I had to be the one to get the story, but he never said I had to write the words myself. I think he's got guys watching me, so I gotta be careful about everything I do. From now on, watch your back."

Tony took another sip of his drink and continued.

"That first tape is all about where it began. He talked about his life like he'd died as a kid and was reborn as this grade A asshole. He spoke a lot about the house he grew up in. He didn't give me the address of the house where he grew up though, so I still need to look that up, but I'm gonna see if the house is still there. This guy is all over the system. Any chance you can track down his parents—find out if they are still alive? He told me that he killed his dad, but something tells me that is all bullshit. Maybe he's got brothers or sisters? Get back to me if you find anything." Tony instructed as he gulped the last of his drink. It was show time.

Bobby entered San Francisco Chronicle editor Carol Gibson's office unannounced, without even as much as a knock, with tape recorder in hand. Bobby had a look of fear on his face as he stared at Carol, placing the tape recorder on her desk and clicking play.

"Carol you've got to hear this for yourself. This is Tony's interview from today with that killer Ramirez. Listen." Bobby said.

The two listened intently until they heard Tony's voice over the crackling of the background noise.

"It's Tuesday, October 18, 2011. I'm interviewing serial killer Reynaldo Ramirez from Death Row in San Quentin Prison. Ramirez is due to be executed in five days. These interviews are source material for a series in the Chronicle to run up and through his final days. So, Ramirez, the tape is running. You wanted me here, so tell your story."

"I was born on October 31, 1966 in Tijuana, Mexico. My parents immigrated here when I was 3. Mom stayed home Dad worked doing whatever he could when he wasn't drunk. I was 5 or 6, I figured out what living with a drunk really was. When my father would come home I was always sent to my room. If I didn't hear any yelling, I was allowed to come out and see him. If I heard yelling, which was most nights, I was to stay in my room. Night after night, I would hear my mother take her beating and then serve dinner to that asshole. I spent the last 15 plus years thinking about it, and I'm pretty sure it was those nights that allowed me to become who I was to become. Night after night, I dreamed about killing my

father for what he did to my mom. She never defended herself and I wasn't old enough to do anything about it. My mom didn't tell anyone, even though that meant hiding from her friends. My mom kept me inside most of the time since we lived near the blacks. By the time I was in junior high, our neighborhood was overrun with blacks. If you weren't black, you were a target. We couldn't afford to move—my dad spent whatever was left over on booze and women.

One day on my way home, I found a cat that had been hit by a car—dead in the street. I still remember how fresh the kill was. I sat there on the sidewalk, poking it with a stick, fantasizing about how it had died and how it must have felt at the moment of impact. I found myself staring at the insides of the cat, and was frustrated that I hadn't gotten to witness its death. I knew I had to fix that.

When I was 13, we had this stray cat that would always come into our yard and meow in heat and shit everywhere. My mom would try to chase it off with a broom, but I had a better idea for that damn cat. One day I was home from school, and my mom was out of the house when I found that cat sniffing around the yard. I lured the cat to me with some food. When she came close enough, I picked her up. I held her up and looked her straight in the eyes. I pet her behind the ears, then on her neck. She had no idea that I was about to chock the life out of her until it was too late. As I squeezed her throat shut I could see fear in her eyes. She was afraid of **me**. She scratched me like a son of a bitch but I didn't care. I kept squeezing until her legs went limp and the life seeped out of her body and her eyes went blank. It was the first time I felt power over the life or death of something and I loved it. It was such a rush! Most people will never know what that is. I knew right then I needed more. Something bigger."

"You got off strangling a cat? You felt power killing an animal smaller than you?"

"You act like you never killed anything Tony. A bug? A spider? Killing is human nature, man. To deny it is to deny God. I would never deny God."

"Yeah, you wouldn't want to do that. Go on."

"I killed countless shit over the next year. Buried them where I could. One afternoon this fucking dog kept barking all day long. I was home sick that day and that damn dog would not shut the hell up. I got out of bed, grabbed a hotdog out of the fridge and lured that damn dog into the backyard. As it ate, I pummeled its skull with a shovel. That dog yelped and ran around in circles, all confused and shit. It was funny to me. I finally crushed its head in so it would stop running around. Unfortunately my father got home before I could clean it up. He stumbled in the house drunk off his ass at noon and passed out on the couch. That evening when he woke up, he found some of the dog's brains on our back porch. He flew off the handle, and hit me and accused me of killing some animal. It wasn't hard to find where I buried the dog. He came unglued. It was I think the first time in years he actually paid attention to what the hell I was doing."

"How old where you?"

"Fourteen. He wanted to know what had happened, so I told him. No remorse, no excuses. At that moment, I knew then and there—who I was and what I wanted to do. The power was too great to ignore. He hit me again and again, calling me names and shit. I didn't care. I was at peace. My mom got between us and she tried to stop him. She was screaming at him to stop. He didn't care and did what came naturally to him—he smacked her to the ground and started yelling at her. As he focused on her, my blood began to boil. Without a thought, I slipped behind him, got the shovel and smashed his head in. I felt his skull collapse under the weight of my strike. As he fell to his knees, he looked up at me. Do you believe the asshole actually had a look of confusion on his face? It was like he had no idea what the hell was going on. Talk about living in denial. I think in the time it took me to raise that shovel up over my head and bring it down on his pathetic face, he might have been more sober than he'd been in years. I didn't give a shit. Just as easy as you'd crush a bug, I slammed that shovel into his brains. His head *exploded like a watermelon. It was fucking amazing. I don't think my mom experienced it like I did, but she got that he wouldn't be hitting us anymore. That was good enough for her. Together we buried his ass with that mangy mutt. From then on, I couldn't wait for the day I could leave home and have people fear my name."*

Chapter 7

Tony pulled up to a house in a neighborhood full of run-down low-rent housing. Hunters' Point had been a mecca for urban decay since the '60s and '70s complete with sky-high rates of unemployment and crime. There had been dozens of plans to renovate the area, but in the current economy it had been left to its continued decomposition. Tony watched two black boys kicking cans down the street swearing at three black teenage girls.

Ramirez's house looked abandoned—the windows were boarded up, and gangs had tagged them relentlessly. The yard was a dirt lot, and the porch sagged at one end, clearly needing to be replaced. A "Condemned" sign had been stapled to the door.

Tony got out of the truck and walked up to the front steps, aware that he was being watched by a group of young black teens across the street. He stepped carefully around broken glass, cans, and scattered clothing on the porch and ground. He peered inside the house through an opening between some of the boards. It appeared that the house had been used most recently by local addicts and homeless folks.

Tony's cell phone rang in his jacket pocket.

"This is Tony."

"Hey, Tone. It's Bobby. Got some information for you. I found the mom. She's up at St. Francis Memorial Hospital." Bobby reported.

"You found her?"

"Yeah, wasn't that hard. Her kid's getting the needle in a few days. The Examiner did an interview with her. It ran last week. Anyway, no siblings either."

"Ok, thanks." Tony said, ending the call and pocketing the phone.

Tony walked back towards his truck, now host to the group of teens that had been watching him. "I was just leaving." Tony said to the kid he believed to be the leader, as he climbed into the driver's seat.

"Yeah, I bet you were."

The trip to St. Francis was a short seven mile drive north on the 101 towards Chinatown. The hospital had been built in 1905—and promptly burned to the ground the following year during the 1906 earthquake. In 1911, the hospital re-opened with 100 beds, and had expanded through the years. Tony found Ramirez's mother easily, announcing that he was there to do another story on her. The nurses were all too happy to help Mrs. Ramirez be heard. She was well-liked on the unit and the staff felt bad that her son had turned out so poorly. She focused on her memories of her son's youth, before his heart turned black.

Tony entered the room and found Mrs. Ramirez lying in bed, looking out the window. Her sunken eyes, leathery skin, and thinning gray hair showed the effects of a hard life.

"Mrs. Ramirez?" Tony asked quietly.

"¿Que? ¿Quien esta ahí?"

"Mrs. Ramirez? My name is Tony Evans; I'm a...reporter for..."

"¿Otro periodista? ¿Que quieres?"

"Mrs. Ramirez, I'm sorry—my Spanish is really bad." Tony spoke slowly, hoping she'd understand him.

"What do you want? I already talked to you people. I have nothing more to say." Mrs. Ramirez responded.

"I'm sorry, Mrs. Ramirez—I'm not from the Examiner. My name is Tony Evans. My daughter, Nicole was kidnapped last night. You may have seen it on the TV?"

Mrs. Ramirez focused her eyes on Tony as he pulled a chair beside her bed. Without moving, Mrs. Ramirez responded sympathetically.

"Si, Si. I saw it on TV. I'm sorry but I can't help you."

"Mrs. Ramirez, I think you can. You see, I'm doing a story on your son, and he spoke a great deal about you and his childhood. That's why I'm here. I believe your son is responsible for my daughter's kidnapping, and that I am supposed to speak with you." Tony pleaded.

"Mi hijo is responsible you say?" Mrs. Ramirez looked away and paused. "I'm sorry for your loss."

"No, no—I don't think you understand. My daughter is still alive, and I really need to find her."

"You say mi hijo is responsible? Then your daughter is not alive—she's gone. Mi hijo es el diablo."

"Yes, ma'am. I know all about your son. But, for some reason, I think he's kept her alive so I'll do him a favor. I need to understand more about him, about how he became so twisted so I can find my daughter before he has her killed."

"How is that going to help? Why you make me remember?"

"Maybe if I understand him better, I'll be able to figure out where he's taken her. I know where Reynaldo grew up, but it doesn't look like she's there. What about his father? Maybe he had her taken there. Where can I find him?"

"I'm old. I have cancer. Just let me be." Mrs. Ramirez cut him off.

"His father, Mrs. Ramirez—where can I find him?"

"In the ground." Mrs. Ramirez responded coldly.

"Dead? You're saying he's dead?"

"Si. He was the first you know." Mrs. Ramirez confessed.

"The first? What do you mean?" Tony asked excitedly.

"Reynaldo got tired of him beating us. His dad was a drunk with a mean streak. He loved to beat on us." She explained. "I don't want to talk about such things."

"Please, Mrs. Ramirez. It's important. What else do you remember about that day?"

"My husband was not a nice person. He drank and beat me all the time. Rey was all I had. Rey wanted to protect me. All we had was each other. I know what my son is, but I always loved him." Mrs. Ramirez said visibly upset.

"I understand Mrs. Ramirez."

"He found a dead dog that Rey killed. I don't know why Rey did it, but my husband was angry and started screaming and beating my son. He kept calling him el Diablo and other horrible things. He was only 14—just a boy. I screamed at him to stop, and he started hitting me. He pushed me to the ground and kept beating me. Then next thing I remember was my husband's head bleeding all over me. Rey stood over me with that shovel in his hands and then pulled me up from the ground. As soon as I was steady on my feet, Rey turned back to my husband's body and started swinging away. I will never forget that sight." Mrs. Ramirez cried at the memory.

"You mean Ramirez was telling the truth? He was not embellishing his killings?" said Tony apologetically. "What did the police do?"

"¿Policía? No, no policía where we lived. We take care of our own. I helped him bury my husband that night and told everyone that he left for another woman. That happens. I always knew Rey was different. I tried to love him. I really tried, but I failed him. Rey left home at 17, and part of me was glad. I didn't hear from him again for many, many years, until he was arrested."

"His father truly was his first....kill?"

"Si. First person he killed. I've never told anyone that before. I know there were others afterwards. I never told anyone, out of fear he would kill me if I did. When he left, that was the best thing for me. But every day I was afraid he would come back looking for me, 'cuz I knew his secrets."

"He can't hurt you anymore, Mrs. Ramirez."

"I confess my sins, for my own salvation, Mr. Evans. God will judge me, and I pray for His mercy. Now leave me. That house and my son were filled with evil. Leave me, and let me live out my last days in peace."

Under the cover of moon light, Tony pulled his truck up to Ramirez's childhood home in Hunter's Point and turned off the lights. He sat patiently in the darkness waiting for his eyes to adjust to the night, curious what kind of activity might be going on in the neighborhood at this hour. All was quiet—maybe even too quiet. Tony pulled a flashlight from his glove compartment and tested the batteries. Satisfied, Tony got out of the truck and opened his trunk. He glanced at his watch and saw that it was just past 3:00 a.m. He smiled to himself as he pulled a shovel from his trunk—he would never have believed that he'd be digging up bodies in the middle of the night.

Tony walked towards the backyard, using the flashlight to light his way. When Tony reached the fence, he opened the wooden gate and slipped inside the yard, closing the creaky gate behind him. Switching on his flashlight, Tony started searching for anything out of the ordinary, not exactly sure what he was looking for. Tony's beam of light covered the base of the abandoned house, and backyard, stopping on dry withering trees and long forgotten plants. The brown grass and plants were as dead as the house. Walking slowly around the property, Tony continued to look for any signs of life. In the back corner of the lot, something finally caught his eye. While most of the yard's dirt was packed tight, the earth in the back corner looked as if it had been disturbed. Tony began to shovel. Nearly an hour later, the shovel struck something hard. Clawing through the dirt with his hands, Tony uncovered a metallic box the size of a small lunch pail. He pried the box open and found a folded note and a Polaroid. To his horror, Tony stared at a photo of his daughter, hands and ankles bound with duct tape, on her knees. She was wearing only a man's flannel shirt and her eyes were covered with a bandana. It looked as if her face had been forced into some kind of dog dish, further demoralizing her. Choking back tears and enraged at what this monster was doing to his little girl, Tony dropped the picture back into the box and grabbed the note.

> **"So you found my old man. You're one step closer to the girl. Bring this to me. Tick tock."**

The letter was in a basic courier font and could have been printed anywhere. Tony saw nothing unusual about the note, not even the paper it was printed on. He tossed it back into the box with the photo and shut the lid. Considering what the note said, Tony shed light into the hole again, wondering if there was anything more here for him. Light glinted off a white object protruding from the dirt. After a few minutes of digging, Tony extracted a human femur bone from the hole he'd made.

"SHIT!" Tony shouted, as he tossed the bone back into the hole, and scrambled backwards.

Chapter 8

Though it felt like his eyes would never open, Tony became aware that the sun was beginning to beam into his room. Still clad in his grave digging gear, he pushed himself up from the bed, and started towards the door. The paper had likely already been delivered. Throwing open the deadbolt, Tony grabbed the paper and returned inside to his kitchen table with it. As he unfolded the paper, the front page headline screamed out at him:

"Serial Killer in His Own Words, Part 1: A Series by Tony Evans."

Tony breathed a sigh of relief and spoke aloud to the silent room, "Oh, Thank GOD, Bobby! YES!"

Tony brewed some coffee, took a quick shower, then scanned Bobby's article. It was all there. Satisfied, he kicked into high gear so he could get back out to the prison for his next interview.

Tony was already in his wooden chair, tape recorder at the ready, waiting to start the interview when Ramirez entered the cage in the interview room. As before, Ramirez did not take his eyes off Tony while the guards were chaining his legs to the floor. When they were finished with their procedures, they left the room loudly bolting the door.

"I see you got my story in the paper. I knew you'd do it. So... did you find my father?" Ramirez asked.

Tony pulled the Polaroid from his jacket pocket and held it up in the air to show Ramirez.

"Ahhh—you found the old man! Maybe you are the right person to tell my tale."

"I want my daughter, you sick bastard!" Tony screamed. "I played your game. Now tell me where she is!" Tony demanded.

"Doesn't work that way, man. You'll get her back when all the stories I have to tell are in print."

"Unharmed!" Tony instructed.

"If you play by my rules…" Ramirez replied coldly.

"Now—you ready for today's story? You have some writing to do!" said Ramirez.

Later that day, Tony made his way through the Chronicle news bullpen like he was on a mission. Tony ignored the confused looks of those who were aware that he'd been laid off and navigated his way through the maze of cubicles to reach Bobby's desk.

"Hey! Here's today's tape. Ramirez seemed happy with your article." Tony reported.

"That's great, Tone! What's on that new tape? " Bobby asked sarcastically.

"He talked a lot about his wife and her lover."

"Wife and lover?" Bobby repeated confused.

"Apparently his wife got tired of his bizarre behavior and looked elsewhere to get her needs met. Ramirez found them in the act. Beat the crap out of her and tortured the guy while she watched. He smiled the whole time he told the story. This sick bastard is TWISTED!" Tony exclaimed.

Bobby grimaced as he imagined Ramirez's brutality.

"Lovely, huh? It's all on the tape. As much as he talked about what he did to them, he wouldn't give me much more than names. I need you to leverage research, and have them go through the archives and any other means to find out who these people were. Ramirez left me a "package" at his parents' place yesterday. If he follows the same pattern, we'll need to know where to look for the next clue! Call me as soon as you get something."

"I'll get right on it. Where're you going to be?" Bobby asked.

"I'm headed over to Amy's. Call me!" Tony said as he headed towards the door.

"Tony!"

Tony scanned the cube city for the owner of the voice. Carol Gibson looked worried as she stepped out of her office and met his eyes. She reached out to embrace him.

"I'm so sorry about all of this. Is there any news about Nicky? We're doing whatever we can here to help. If you need anything, ANYTHING at all you let me know. I'll do whatever I can." offered Carol sympathetically.

"I appreciate that, Carol. Thanks for all you've done. I need to get going though. I just came by to drop off Bobby's next tape." Tony responded as he turned towards the exit.

"Wait a minute! There are some people in my office that stopped by to see you." Carol said, concern seeping through.

"What people?" Tony asked.

Carol opened her door, exposing the awaiting occupants. Tony scowled as he recognized the police detectives.

"Agent Lorenzo Callcut." Tony stated.

"Mr. Evans—so glad you could fit us into your busy schedule. You're a hard man to locate." Callcut said.

"What do you want?"

"Whoa, hold on cowboy! I just need to ask you a few questions about your missing daughter."

"You got any leads?"

"We're working on a few things but you dodged me the other day. You didn't tell me the whole truth back at your in-laws' place did you?" Callcut accused.

"I told you what I knew, and that was nothing. I went to work and came home, watched the news, went to see Amy, talked to you, and came home and went to bed. What did I miss?" Tony said annoyed.

"You didn't go to work because you have no job. You've been out to San Quentin. What are doing in the Pen the evening your kid vanishes? You're not a reporter anymore, what are you up to? Who'd you go to see?"

"What, Callcut, don't you read the papers? I'm doing my job—I'm a reporter—and always will be. What difference to your investigation does it make where I work, or what I'm writing? Seems to me that if you were chasing leads instead of me, you'd be closer to finding her!"

"Hold up! I've got people working on the leads we have. You, well, I'm working this angle. Besides you didn't answer my question." Callcut poked, trying to get a rise out of Tony.

"It's all in the paper. You're a cop, you figure it out. I got shit to do. Are we done here?" Tony asked angrily.

"For now. Don't go too far though." Callcut replied.

Bobby sat down at his desk and stared at the tape sitting on his desk. Images from yesterday's interview played in his mind, despite his disgust with the content. Reluctantly, Bobby opened the top drawer of his desk and pulled the headphones out of his iPod. He inserted the new tape into the recorder on his desk and slipped his headphones on. After a short pause, Bobby heard Tony's voice.

"It's Wednesday, October 19,, 2011. I'm interviewing serial killer Reynaldo Ramirez from Death Row. Ramirez is due to be executed in four days. You told me about killing your father yesterday; what is it that you want to tell me today?"

"Today we're gonna talk about my wife."

"Go ahead then."

"I met Mia when I was twenty-three. She was pretty—even for a stripper. One night I was roaming—looking for something to get

into. It had been quite some time since I'd indulged in some real fun. At that time, I didn't have a job and I got by breaking into homes and grabbing what I could. I would pocket the cash and sell the shit I could get my hands on. Anyway I was leaving a bar one night, and some guy was slapping the shit out of this girl. I was a little drunk and angry for some reason; I don't remember why—I was just in a foul mood. This guy kept hitting this girl, and as I went up to them, I told him to leave her alone. He made the mistake of telling me to fuck off. I should have killed that shit-bag right then and there, but she wouldn't have it. I punched him until his face was a bloody mess and she started screaming at me to stop. She was grateful that I dragged him off her, so she took me to her place. She cleaned my hands and then took me to her bed. I should have known how easy she was. She said it was her way of thanking me. Wish I'd known how many men she'd shown her "gratitude" to in bed. I thought she was perfect for me, and we got married a few months later."

"She married you because you stopped a fight?"

"She MARRIED ME because she LOVED ME! To this day I know I had her heart. The bitch just could not keep her legs closed. She went out a lot at night, which worked for me as I did, too, but for very different reasons.

I went to L.A. to get away from possible heat in the Bay area in the 90's and to do a little hunting."

"Hunting?"

"I needed my fix. It was getting harder and harder to watch her lay in bed at night naked and knowing how easy it would be to suffocate her then gut her. She was a stripper—no one would have missed her. I had a hundred reasons to see her dead, but there was something about her that calmed me. That bitch drove me crazy. Anyway, I went away to "visit friends in LA" for a few weeks, and she didn't give me any shit about it or nothing. We worked well in that way. When I had fulfilled my thirst for death, I came back, to find that she'd been banging some other guy in our bed. That was it. I knew then and there she had to die. I followed the guy for a few days. He'd meet her at the club and then they'd go to his place. And get this shit; she'd still want to have sex with me when she got in, even after spending hours with him! That's bullshit! When I told her I knew, she bounced. She already had a bag stowed in her car. Didn't take me long to find out where she was. She moved around a lot, but I'd always find her.

One day, I found her living in an apartment house in Oakland. You know one of those big houses with lots of rooms that are rented out? Anyway I watched the place for a while and found out that not many of the rooms were rented. That night, she was only in the house with that guy, and I broke in. I found a crescent wrench in a junk drawer in the kitchen and climbed the stairs in silence. I slipped into her room unnoticed and watched as he pumped away on top of her. He never saw it coming as I slammed that wrench into his head. I popped her one to shut her up.

I dragged him off of her and tied his naked body to a chair. He wasn't all that impressive. I don't see what she saw in him. I grabbed a chair from another room, placed it just across from him, and then tied her to it. I began working him, making sure she saw every bit of pain I inflicted on this little man; for all the hurt she caused me. When I finally crushed his testicles with my wrench, I think she knew how it felt when she left me. That guy was nothing but a blubbering, bloody, broken pile of crap when I was done. When I finally got tired of him, I split his skull open and let his brains drip on to the floor. At the end, she begged me to kill her. I helped her out. I took my time when I squeezed the last life from her lungs, staring deep into her eyes like that cat all those years ago. You know there really is no difference when a person and an animal die. Their eyes just fade away.'"

"You're a sick motherfucker, Ramirez. I can't listen to this shit anymore."

Tony drove the city streets back to his apartment, frantically checking his watch. He needed to get his act together. The morning had burned away from him and he was now late to meet Amy. Tony fumed about Callcut's unspoken accusation that he had anything to do with Nicky's disappearance. She was his LIFE—if he lost her, he didn't know how he'd cope.

Turning the corner Tony found an open parking spot on the street just two blocks down from his apartment. He jumped out and raced towards his apartment. Reaching the security gate, Tony punched in his code and bolted up the stairs. At the top of the landing, Amy stood, arms crossed.

"Amy! Sorry I'm late! I got held up at the paper." Tony exclaimed, desperately trying to catch his breath.

"It's fine, Tony. I just got here myself. You ok?" Amy asked politely.

"I'm ok—just beat. Those damn stairs..." Tony said unlocking his apartment door. "Come on in."

Amy followed Tony inside the sparse apartment. She looked around at the disarray. Tony hadn't made any headway in cleaning the place up since her departure. Even the sink was still piled with dishes.

"Can I get you something to drink? Coffee? Water? Lumpy milk?" Tony asked as he sloshed the chunks around in the carton.

"No, I'm fine." Amy replied as she sat down on the couch.

Tony microwaved a cup of coffee from the morning's now cold pot. Cup in hand, he joined Amy on the couch. Tony noticed the deep black circles under Amy's eyes and wanted to put his arms around Amy and comfort her. Unsure of what would be right; Tony stood instead and paced around the room, sipping his coffee.

"Have you heard anything from the police?" Tony started.

"You haven't spoken to them yet?" Amy replied, disappointed.

"No—I mean, yes—I spoke with Agent Callcut this morning." Said Tony defensively.

"I'm sorry. I didn't mean...I'm...I'm just so tired and drained. I just want my baby back. Who could have done something so evil?" Amy cried, using her hands to hide her tears.

"Baby, I'm so sorry."

Tony puts his coffee down on the coffee table and took Amy in his arms. She sobbed as he sat, silently trying to hold back his own tears.

"I know baby. I know. I want her back, too. We'll get her back. I promise." Tony said softly.

"How? How can you promise that? You can't! Don't you dare tell me that she'll be ok! You have NO idea!" Amy lashed out as she pulled away from Tony.

"Honey, no, I just....I just have a feeling." offered Tony.

"What? What do you know?" Amy questioned, becoming increasingly suspicious of Tony. "What did you DO Tony?!"

"Me? No—Amy, I didn't do anything. Listen—listen to me! I didn't want to upset you, but I have something you need to know." Tony said, preparing for his confession.

Tony reached out and grasped Amy's hands and disclosed the events associated with Nicki's kidnapping. He shared with her the details of the interviews, and even of his midnight escapades. After listening quietly for fifteen minutes, Amy pulled away from Tony, and then slapped him hard.

"You knew all along and you didn't tell the cops at my parents place? In FACT, if you had done the story in the first place instead of screwing around this guy never would have taken Nicki! Is that what you're telling me? That you, by just taking a week's job and interviewing this piece of shit like you USED to do for a living, that you could have avoided all of this? And Nicki would be with us? IS THAT WHAT YOU ARE TELLING ME TONY?" Amy screamed.

"Amy, please calm down."

"Calm down? Calm down? You put our daughter in danger. Even if you didn't know it was our daughter, you willingly put SOMEONE's kid in danger."

"I didn't know what he was capable from inside. He's on Death Row for Christ's sake. How was I to know?"

"Because he's Reynaldo Ramirez! You KNOW what he's capable of! He's in jail because he's EVIL! What's wrong with you? Don't you watch National Geographic and all those prison shows? How inmates run neighborhoods from behind bars? I can't believe you would be so nonchalant about a threat like that. If you didn't believe he could carry out his threat, then why didn't you just tell the cops before you left?"

"Amy, I don't, I don't know. I..."

"Have you told Callcut?" "No."

"No? What, are you crazy?" Amy screamed.

"No, I'm not crazy. I can't tell the cops because we KNOW he has her. I think he may have people following me now. I have to play his bullshit game. He's demanding that I follow these clues to get her back. If I go to the cops, he'll kill her immediately. I made the mistake of not acting sooner and putting Nicki in this. We WILL get her back, and she WILL be OK!"

"We? Who?" Amy asked.

"The paper's running the stories. I have another journalist writing for me so I can spend my time looking for her. I have the entire research department fact-checking so I can figure out these clues faster. As soon as I have something solid, I'll involve the cops, but not if it can get back to Ramirez. You have to trust me on this. I will not let you or Nicki down!" Pleaded Tony.

"What do you have so far?" Amy asked, calming somewhat.

"I know his game. I solved his little puzzle yesterday. I'm waiting for research to call me and get me an address or a name to start with." Tony said, reaching for Amy again.

"What do you need from me?" Amy asked.

"For you to be with your family. Go to their place and make sure that someone's with you at all times. Are the police still watching the place?"

"Yes."

"Good. You'll be safe there. If I figure out where Nicki's being held, I swear I'll tell the cops. Right now, I need a quick shower to wake up. The paper should be calling soon."

Amy and Tony stood up and hugged tightly. Tony looked deeply into Amy's eyes and kissed her. Amy searched for hope in Tony's face. Amy returned the kiss, sliding her tongue into his mouth longingly. The embrace was broken by ringing from Tony's cell phone.

"Tony here. Yeah, what do you have?" Tony asked, taking notes on the back of an electric bill. "Yes. Got it. I'm on it. Let me know what else you find. Thank you. Keep digging—there must be more."

Chapter 9

Nicki couldn't remember the last time she had felt so hungry. Her head ached from the large bump on the back of her head where he'd hit her. Strapped in the chair, she was unable to take the pressure off that spot, causing a constant reminder of the pain. Her face was swollen and bruised from his blows, but probing by her tongue suggested she still had all her teeth.

The blindfold was tight and resistant to her maneuvering. Nicki strained to listen for sounds of life in the darkness but heard nothing. Her mouth was sour from the gag—a taste she surely didn't want to identify. The duct tape binding her wrists and ankles to the chair had begun to cut into her flesh. She moaned, hoping to get the attention of her kidnappers. She didn't want to upset them again but she needed relief. She learned her lesson the first time when she tried to scream and escape.

"Shut up over there and quit moving around! Do you need to be reminded again who's in control here?" The loud voice silenced Nicki instantly.

"Yeah, I thought so."

Dante Fischer, now even more on edge than before, turned back to stare out the dirty cracked window overlooking the San Francisco waterfront. Dante or Deuce as he was called on the street—had always been someone's second in command. He was six foot three with a slender yet muscular build, long stringy hair, and hadn't shaven or washed for over a week. He stood alert, scanning the shipyard below watching for movement. Dante paused to stare into the corner of the shipyard then reached into his brown camouflage military jacket and withdrew a pair of binoculars. Reassured, he returned the binoculars to his pocket, picked up the can of beans he'd placed on the window sill and resumed eating.

The large warehouse was dilapidated, and broken bottles and furniture lay strewn around making it maze-like. Dante wanted to keep a tactical advantage over anyone that entered the warehouse. A faint creak from the stairwell behind him caught Dante's attention. He silently put his can down and palmed his Glock G17 9 mm pistol, dropping to one knee and targeting on the man climbing the stairs.

"Yo, D! What the hell, man?"

Dante stood up and holstered his weapon to the familiar voice of his partner, Carter Jackson. Carter was much shorter than Dante but easily weighed sixty pounds more. Everyone on the street called Carter "Fat J" as a result. Carter wasn't well-liked by fellow gang members because he was seen as weak. They shoved the shit jobs at him, and Carter put up with it because it allowed him to be *part* of things.

"Yo, D—you feed that girl man?" he asked Dante.

"Fuck her. She'll be dead soon enough." Dante snapped, returning to his post to watch the docks.

"Man, you can't just not feed her man. What is wrong with you?" Fat J pleaded with Dante.

Fat J walked to the far corner, frustrated with Dante's lack of compassion for their hostage. He stared at Nicki for a moment, disheveled and bound to the chair, then grabbed a can of Chef Boyardee Beefaroni and a plastic fork from a bag on the floor. Fat J popped the top off the can then reached out to pull the bandana gag from Nicki's mouth. Nicki resisted the urge to scream and instead opened her mouth in response to the smell of the cold food.

"What the hell are you doing?!" Dante screamed at Fat J, running up behind him, spinning him around and punching him in the face. Fat J reeled backwards and crashed into some old furniture stacked in the corner. Before Fat J could reach for his weapon, Dante was on top of the large man, Glock drawn and the barrel of the weapon buried in the Fat J's temple.

"You touch that bitch again, to feed her, or anything else and I will drop your fat ass. Do you understand me?" Dante sneered.

"Man that is some bullshit! You can't just..."

"Yes! Yes, I can. And I will and so will you. She drinks what I give her, and that's it. She can shit herself for all I care. She's gonna suffer and then she's gonna die. Don't you grow a fucking conscience and bitch out at go time. If I have to, I'll take your ass out, too. You got me?"

"Yeah man, I get it. Now get the damn gun outta my face."

Dante looked at the fallen man for a moment then holstered his weapon. Nicki sobbed and shook involuntarily from her place in the corner. Dante walked over to her, put his hand under her chin, and whispered sadistically in her ear.

"Too bad you're not older. We coulda had ourselves a good time!"

He ran his thumb roughly over her bruised and cracked lips. Nicki tried to pull her head back from Dante's touch but couldn't move. Before she could speak, Dante shoved the gag back in her mouth, spun her chair away from him, and gave it a kick so that it rolled into the corner of the room. As the chair slammed into the cement wall, Nicki screamed, blood now pouring from her knee. Dante chuckled and returned to his post.

"Now get your fat ass down to the shooting gallery. The bitch's father should figure it out soon enough. Get some eyes on him and watch him."

Chapter 10

The Flood Building was one of the more magnificent landmarks in the San Francisco downtown area. At twelve stories tall, the building came to a point between Powell and Market Streets giving it the appearance of a triangle. Built in 1904, the building had survived fires, earthquakes and even the threat of demolition. The building had been repurposed over the years and was now home to over 250 tenants, including large corporate entities like Gap and Urban Outfitters, but also housed a variety of local professionals like Lita Ward and Associates.

After scouring the directory, Tony rode the elevator to the third floor. He found Lita's office easily and approached her receptionist.

"Good morning, sir. Do you have an appointment?" The tall blonde asked.

"Hi. Yes, good morning. I need to speak with Lita Ward. It's very important."

"Yes, of course. Do you have an appointment?"

"No, I don't have an appointment, but like I said, it's extremely important that I speak with her. I just need 10 minutes or so." Tony said, trying not to sound desperate.

"I see. Well, sir, you'll need an appointment and I'm afraid Ms. Ward has a pretty tight schedule today. I have an opening in two weeks at 3pm. Will that work for you?" The young receptionist asked as she scanned the electronic appointment calendar.

"No, that will NOT work. I must speak with her now. It's urgent!" Tony begged.

"Of course. Have a seat, and I'll check with Ms. Ward to see if she can spare a few minutes between clients."

"Thanks—appreciate it." Tony offered, taking a seat in one of the deep wingback chairs.

Tony waited impatiently in the lobby. When the receptionist rose from her desk and headed for the Ladies room, Tony moved closer to the security door—that which separated those who were waiting from those that worked in the inner confines of the suite. As Tony studied the security panel from his chair, a young man entered from the hall. He was unkempt and dressed in torn jeans and a wrinkled shirt that looked as if it had just been pulled out of a hamper. He sat in the chair opposite Tony, but made no eye contact. The tension in the silent lobby was broken by a young attorney who came through the security door.

"Mr. Waters? Come on back." The attorney addressed the rumpled young man.

Tony stood at the same time as did Mr. Waters, stretching his arms out and exhaling, as if exhausted by the waiting process. As the attorney escorted the client through the door, Tony's foot slid out to prohibit the door from closing all the way. He watched as the two men entered an office down the hall, and then slipped through the security door moved quickly down the hallway, scanning the names on the doors for Lita Ward. Several doors down, Tony scored. Hand on the door, and realizing that he'd be interrupting someone else's precious time, he entered.

"Excuse, me? Who are you and what do you think you're doing here?" Lita barked.

"Excuse me. I'm very sorry to interrupt, Ms. Ward, but my name is Tony Evans and I really must speak to you immediately!"

The couples sitting near her desk stared at him confused, unsure whether to rise from their seats or stay put. "Mr. Evans, make an appointment like everyone else! Now OUT!" Lita screamed at Tony.

"Ms. Ward, you don't understand! I MUST speak with you! I don't mean you any harm." Tony offered.

As Tony stood with his back to the door and his hands in surrender position, a security officer entered the room. In a moment the officer had Tony pinned to the ground with his hands cuffed behind him. The officer yanked Tony back onto his feet and pushed him towards the door.

"Ms. Ward my daughter has been kidnapped! She'll die without your help!" Tony pleaded as he moved towards the door.

"That's enough, Mr. Evans! You're obviously ill. Get him out of here!" Lita commanded.

"WAIT! Reynaldo Ramirez has her! You helped his wife, now please, help ME!" Tony begged.

"What did you say?" Lita asked as she put a hand up for the guard to stop.

"Reynaldo Ramirez. You helped his wife once, before she was killed. You were on the prosecutor's team during Ramirez's last trial. Ramirez had my daughter kidnapped. He told me that if I wrote his story, he'd let her live. He's been feeding me clues to her whereabouts during each interview I have with him. I need information about his wife—those details may mean life over death for my daughter!

"What did you say your name was?" Lita asks.

"Evans—Tony Evans."

"Sit him down at that table please." She instructed the guard. "Mr. and Mrs. Anderson, can you please follow Ms. McLain to the conference room? I'll be there in a few minutes." She asked the couple near her desk. "Ms. McLain, please show the Andersons to Conference Room A and provide them with some refreshments. I'll be there in a few minutes" Lita instructed the receptionist waiting in the hallway.

"And can you wait outside the door?" Lita asked the guard. "You can leave Mr. Evans cuffed." She added.

As the office emptied, Lita Ward moved to her desk and leaned against it. She removed her glasses and stared at Tony. Her black and grey power suit accentuated her athletic build and long blonde hair, and emanated power and control. While deeply uncomfortable in the handcuffs, Tony waited patiently for Lita to speak.

"Mr. Evans, I'll give you five minutes before I ask that security officer to get back in here and bounce you out of this building. What is all this about?"

"My sources tell me that when you were at the Prosecutors office you investigated a complaint from Mia Ramirez. Is that correct?" Tony started.

"Your sources? Do you work for the papers? TV?"

"No—yes—I did until last week. Listen—did you read the Chronicle this morning? Did you read the story about the little girl that was missing?"

"Yes, I glanced over the article."

"That's my daughter, Nicki. Reynaldo's men have her."

"He's being executed midnight Sunday, isn't he?" Lita asked.

"Yes—so I have to find her before then or she'll die too. I've got to get more information about his late wife Mia and I've been coming up empty. You're my last shot."

"What do you want to know?"

"I'm not really sure. Maybe you can start by telling me a little bit more about her case—the one you investigated."

"There's not much to tell: Mia came to our office, complaining that the police weren't doing anything about her situation."

"What situation?" Tony asked. He tried to turn towards her, to sit more naturally, but every movement sent pain through his back and shoulders as the cuffs restrained him. "Any chance I could have these things taken off?"

Lita opened the door and asked the guard to come in. The guard removed the cuffs, pocketed the key and returned to his watch post outside the door. Lita walked to the conference table and sat and invited Tony to do the same. Tony reached into his jacket pocket and removed his small tape recorder.

"Do you mind if I record our conversation?" Tony asked.

"Only if you don't run any of this in the paper." Lita replied.

"Agreed. What was the situation that Mia came to you about?" Tony asked, pressing the record button as he placed the device on the table.

"Mia came to us because she was angry that the police wouldn't do anything about Ramirez. She said that he beat her. Frankly, she had a black eye when she came in, so it seemed believable to me. I checked with the police, and they took her statement. Apparently, although a detective was assigned to the case, he never caught up with Ramirez. Ramirez came and went as he pleased, and he wasn't working so there was no rhyme or reason to his movements. The police staked out their apartment for a while, but after a few days and no luck, they moved on to other cases. On the follow-up, Mia withdrew the complaint. I figured she'd probably gotten scared of what he'd do to her when he found out that she'd filed a complaint—pretty classic in battered women's cases. Last time I spoke to her, she told me that she was moving out and divorcing Ramirez."

"Do you know where she moved?"

"Some place off of MLK Way. I'd have to look it up."

"Did you ever see the place?"

"Yeah, it was a real dump, but it was all she could afford. It was one of those great big homes outfitted as a boarding house. When I did my last follow-up with her, she said she hadn't seen Ramirez in months and she was seeing some guy. Tommy something or other" Lita said.

"Tommy Reid."

"Reid! Yes, that was his name. She wasn't divorced yet but she said that she didn't think Reynaldo would be back. A month or two later, we hear that Mia and Tommy were the victims of a double homicide. We always figured Ramirez was good for it." Lita recalled.

"Why didn't you drag him in? Your office didn't charge him?"

"The Prosecutor chose not to. The police department didn't make any arrests. Witnesses at the house validated that she'd been seeing Tommy but they also noted that they'd seen her with another man as well shortly before her murder. The police picked him up and cleared him. He had no priors and was cooperative—he even had an alibi. I think he worked at a local restaurant or something. The investigation remained open till we got Reynaldo on the other murder, then we closed the case. I left the Prosecutor's office a year or two later and have been in private practice ever since."

"How'd they die?" Tony asked, wanting to know if Lita had any further information than what Ramirez had shared.

"Police found a wrench at the scene. It looked like the killer used it to beat them with it. There was such rage in that scene. I don't think I will ever get those images out of my head. The walls were covered in the victim's blood. If I remember right, she lived upstairs, last door on the left. There was no evidence of the window being tampered with. Both bodies were naked tied to chairs facing each other. Coroner counted thirty-two separate strikes on Mia's skull—her brains were nearly pulverized when he was done. Tommy took around forty blows to the head and genitals. His balls were crushed to soup. For someone to walk in and bludgeon two people to death the attacker would have been covered in their blood. There was no one else home at the time but no neighbors or anyone heard or saw a thing." Lita recounted.

"Do you have the address of that crime scene?" Tony asked Lita.

"I can get it for you. Give me a minute." Lita said as she reached for her phone.

Chapter 11

Tony pulled to a stop along Twenty Fifth Street, just off of Martin Luther King Jr. Way. The start of the sun's late afternoon descent into the West told Tony that he only had a few hours of light left, and he had to get what he needed and get out of this area before night fall. East Oakland had long had a history of gang violence and had topped the statistical charts for crime. In 1984 Grove Street was renamed Martin Luther King Jr. Way and had historically represented the dividing line of the neighborhoods where minorities could and could not rent or buy property. In 2008, East and West Oakland made up 72% of all violent crime in Oakland, though these areas were only inhabited by 44% of the population. Today, MLK Way divides Oakland from neighboring Berkeley, and represents one the most impoverished areas of the East Bay.

Tony parked his Highlander and looked around, wondering what the hell he was doing here. He was beginning to wish that he had taken Amy's advice to let Callcut in on everything and let *him* do the investigating. Having a black man, a black cop, no less, might have proven very helpful in an area like this. As a reporter, Tony generally declined stories in areas like these.

Tony sat staring at the crumbling building that looked as if it were moments away from being condemned. The building's exterior was plastered with posters announcing one thing or another, cigarette butts were strewn everywhere and there was broken glass from the light poles—no longer providing the safety of a lit street. Gang spray-painted graffiti fought for dominance on the boarded-up windows and walls. No fewer than six abandoned cars and an old boat rusted in the lot behind the building. Addicts climbed through holes in the fence along the lot and made their way into the building from an entrance in the back. Tony struggled with his desire to put his Highlander in gear and high-tail it out of there, but knew that his daughter's life might depend on his entering the building.

As he contemplated what lay before him, two black hookers made their way onto the scene. Dressed in shiny tube tops and short shorts, they teetered on 7-inch heels, hawking their wares to every passing car. One woman was nearly 6 feet tall, skinny as a rail, with medium but firm breasts, that were pushed up and threatening to spill out of her top. She sported a platinum blonde wig and deep red lipstick. The other prostitute was shorter and heavier, with huge breasts teeming from her tiny shirt. As Tony reached to open his door, a car pulled up to the tall hooker and she leaned in to speak to the driver. Nodding, the pro stood up, pulled her tube top down, exposing her breasts to the driver. The man nodded and she climbed into the car. Moments later, the hooker's head disappeared from view, into the drivers lap.

"You've got to be kidding me." Tony sighed to himself.

Tony leaned back in his seat, pulled out his cell and checked the text message from Lita again. Silently, he prayed that he'd gotten it wrong, that Mia Ramirez's last known address was anywhere other than the building before him, but unfortunately the numbers on the house matched those on his screen. A few more minutes passed and Tony noticed the tall hooker exiting her john's car, screaming obscenities and kicking the back of his car as the driver sped away. He watched as she rejoined her partner on the corner, laughing and swearing and stashing her cash.

"No guts, no glory." Tony muttered to himself as he opened his door.

Tony scurries across the street towards the building and the ladies.

"Yo, hey baby, you looking for a date?" The heavyset woman asked.

"No thanks—not today." Tony replied.

"Oh baby, you'll be sorry! Nice white boy like you—you don't know what you're missing!"

Tony, embarrassed by the very thought of it, moved towards the hole in the fence.

"Aw, shit! You a dope fiend? Keep that limp shit away from me, honey." The heavyset pro called out turning away from Tony.

"Shit! You'd break that white boy!" The tall hooker retorted, turning her attention back to the traffic.

"You know that aint no lie girlfriend!" The heavyset hooker said laughing out loud.

Tony made his way to the back of the building. He noticed a tall man, with long stringy hair that covered most of his face leaning over the hood of a rusted Honda Civic. There was something odd about the man—he was dressed in an old green military jacket and cargo pants and wore black combat boots. Tony turns his attention again to the building as he reaches the back entrance. The building was stained with graffiti, torn clothes were strewn along the ground, and the smell of stale beer, vomit and urine emanated from the house. Fighting back the urge to retch, Tony walked through the multicolored door, holding his nose. Inside the door, a large figure stepped in front of him.

"What the fuck do you want?" boomed the voice.

As Tony's eyes adjusted to the darkened interior, he made out the outline of the large black man blocking his way. The man was more than 300 pounds and had body odor so foul that Tony couldn't help but vomit in his mouth. He struggled to keep the rest of his stomach contents down.

"I'm looking for my cousin." Tony chokes out his lie. "My sister said he comes here to fade."

"Who dat be?"

"Joey. Man Joey." Tony said, pinching his nose shut.

"Don't know no Joey. You best get up out of this motherfucker."

"I can't! I gotta find him. He's been gone a few days. If he isn't here, I'll be in and out in no time. If he's here, and he's still alive, I need to get him to a hospital. If he's dead, well—you don't want to deal with the dead, do you?"

"Fool, look around you. You think I don't deal with the dead? They all dead, they just don't know it yet!"

"Yeah, I guess you do." Tony replied, shaking his head.

"You a cop?"

"No."

"Get 'em up." Before Tony could object, the large man shoved Tony against the wall and patted him down. After a thorough search of his body, the man stepped back.

"You got 10 minutes. Then get the hell out of my pad. Anyone fucks you up, it's not my fault, and watch where you step—again, not my fault." He reminded as he pointed down the hallway.

Tony moved silently down the hallway towards the front of the building. He passed what must have been the dining room at one time, and then noticed bedrooms ahead, their doors no longer intact. In one room, a strung out junkie lay on top of a stained mattress in the corner. She stared back at Tony with empty sunken in eyes. Shaken by her skeleton form and glassy-eyed stare, Tony quickens his step and climbs the front stairs. The steps creak and bend under his weight. At the top of the stairs Tony again reeled from the stench of rotting food and flesh. Every fiber of his being urged him to leave this retched place but the thought of his daughter held in a place possibly worse than this one drove him forward. Tony kept his eyes dead ahead, travelling as quickly as he could to the last door on the left. He pushed the door open, slivers of light illuminating the room through tattered curtains. Tony's first step into the room was followed by a loud crunch. Tony froze, scared that he'd stepped on a syringe. Almost afraid to look, he lifted his foot into the light and looked at the sole of his shoe. The squished guts of a large brown cockroach stained the bottom of his shoe. Disgusted yet relieved, Tony continued into the room. Tony pulled up his shirt to cover his nose, fearing that he'd contract some airborne disease in this fecal, garbage-infested hellhole. Tony pulled his cell phone out of his pocket and used the flashlight app to light the room. He moved towards a mattress in the corner, stepping through garbage and debris. A woman slept beneath one load of trash. The foul odor of rotting flesh and garbage finally overpowered Tony and he reeled to the other side of the room to vomit.

Wiping his chin with his sleeve, Tony looked around the room and spotted a closet. The doors had been removed. In the back corner of the closet, boards had been broken and removed from the floor. Tony dropped to his knees and picked at the hole but found nothing. While the space was large enough to hide something, nothing remained.

"Shit!" Tony exhaled.

Tony stood and flashed the beam around the room. A glint of light caught his attention. Shining the beam at the object, Tony discovered a small metallic box. Tony started towards the box then stops when he realized that the sleeping woman held the box clutched to her chest. Holding his breath, Tony kneeled next to her and reached out for the box. Her hands were grey and rotting, and Tony fell backward as he realized that she was dead. As quickly as he could with care, Tony extracted the box from the corpse.

Tony backed out of the room away from the horror within and opened the tin box. In it is another Polaroid of his daughter. Pocketing her picture and putting the box under his arm, Tony walked quickly through the hallway, down the stairs and towards the back door. Just a few feet from the backdoor, the large black man stepped in front of Tony.

"Find what you looking for?" He asked.

"Yeah—yeah, I did. Oh and by the way, you've got a dead woman upstairs."

"Ahh, Misty! Damn man! That bitch never could hold her shit!" the large man replied as he shoved pasted Tony towards the stairs.

Tony exited the building, breathing deeply, trying to clear all the foul odors from his nasal passages. He quickly made his way to his truck and slid in behind the wheel. Slamming the driver door shut, he pulled the photo from his pocket and looked at it closely for a minute. He started the engine and dialed Bobby's number. Bobby picked up on the 3rd ring.

"This is Bobby."

"Bobby, its Tony, where are you?" Tony asked, concerned.

"Tone! I'm at the paper. I just submitted the article for tomorrow morning. Did you find the place?"

"Yeah, I found it. I've got another picture, so grab someone from Research. I'll be there in about 45 minutes. We've got some work to do." Tony said as he slammed his truck into gear and pulled out into the evening traffic.

Chapter 12

Audrey Tustin and Harvey Tisdell patiently waited in the main conference room at the San Francisco Chronicle. The two of them sat opposite each other at the end of a long oak conference table, studying the photo image projected on the conference room's white screen. Audrey, thirty years old, shorter than her counterpart, had her brunette hair pulled back in a ponytail and wire frame glasses resting on her nose. She was frantically jotting notes down on a yellow legal pad. Harvey, her apprentice, was in his mid-twenties and wore his sandy brown hair in a short crew cut; in hopes that people wouldn't notice that he was balding at such a young age. Harvey was pounding away on his laptop, searching the internet for any information he could find relating to the photo. Even though Harvey and Audrey didn't know Nicki Evans personally, they couldn't help but be disturbed by the image projected on the screen: Nicki Evans gagged and tied to a chair inside a large, old abandoned warehouse. Audrey stood up from her seat to get a closer look at the image, then stepped back, seeing the big picture of this full-color image.

Carol Gibson and Bobby Jenkins walked quickly in to the conference room, Tony only a few steps behind. Tony closed the door to the conference room, even though most of the staff had left for the evening.

"Tony, let me introduce you to Audrey and Harvey—they're from our research department. They've been pitching in here. Guys, Tony Evans: Nicki's dad." Bobby said solemnly.

"And I assume the girl in this photo is Nicki?" Audrey inquired delicately.

"Yes—that's my daughter. What do we know?"

"We've been studying the photo you brought us. Is this the only one you have?" Harvey asked.

"Yeah, that's all that I found. No note this time." Tony offered.

"Looks like she's being held in an abandoned warehouse. We've haven't been able to pinpoint where yet. The girl..." Harvey began.

"Nicki." Tony corrected.

"Sorry. Nicki. She looks like she's been in that chair for quite a while. If we zoom in on her hands." Harvey said as he adjusted the image with the program on his laptop, "her wrists show signs of swelling. You can see how the skin is really red there where she's bound. I'm guessing that she's been trying to loosen the duct tape that's binding her."

"Also, the cans." Audrey pointed out as Harvey adjusted the image to provide a broader view of the items at the foot of Nicki's chair.

"The food cans have been opened. Someone's there with her, feeding her. She's not alone."

"Is that supposed to make me feel better—that she's not alone?" Tony retorted.

"Listen...I'm sorry. I didn't mean anything..." Audrey stumbled, surprised by Tony's sudden hostility.

"How do you plan to locate her?" asked Carol, returning the team's attention to the image on the screen.

"We've been trying to study the buildings behind her." Harvey noted, zooming out to bring into view a more complete version of the location. Harvey manipulated the images once again and zoomed in on one of the warehouse windows behind Nicki.

"I think someone wanted us to see this. That sign there! I'm still trying to figure out what it says, but if we can identify that sign, then we can narrow down warehouses that face similar signs. Unfortunately that window pane covers some of the sign, and the other side is too blurry to make it out." Harvey explained.

"What the hell does that sign say? Can you clean that up at all?" Tony asked as he stood up from his chair and moved closer to the screen.

"It's as sharp as I can get it. Sorry." Harvey replied.

"Have you talked to the police?" Audrey asked. "They have much better equipment, and they can fingerprint the box the photo was in."

"No. Not yet anyway." Tony replied.

"Tony, you may actually have to talk with that cop. We only have three days left." Carol prodded gently.

"I KNOW she only has three days!" Tony barked at Carol.

"What I REALLY need to know is where that BUILDING is!" He screamed at the research team.

"That's what we're trying to tell you, sir. We don't know—at least not yet." Audrey said dejectedly.

"Can you keep working on this tonight?" Tony asked.

"Yes! Yes, of course. We'll find this place, right Harvey?" Audrey prompted, looking over at Harvey. Harvey raised his eyebrows, and then nodded dutifully in response.

"Absolutely." Harvey offered, returning his gaze to the building on the screen.

"Good." Tony replied. "I've got to get some air. I can't think straight in here."

Bobby stopped him at the door and extended a large envelope to Tony.

"Tone, here's the original picture. We scanned it so you can keep this one—perhaps take it to the police? We'll keep working on it but I think it's time we called in the cavalry. We're running out of time."

Tony squinted at Bobby.

"I know. I know. Thanks for your hard work. We're gonna find her. Call me the moment you get anything—I don't care what time it is."

Tony left through the front doors of the San Francisco Chronicle and headed across the street to his truck. It was close to midnight and the pressure was starting to get to Tony. As a reporter, Tony was used to long hours and little sleep, but now that *he* was the story, the added stress and pressure was starting to weigh on him. Tony climbed into his truck and sat there for a moment trying to think, but his brain felt like it was turning into mush. Tony opened his wallet and pulled out Agent Callcut's business card and considered calling him. Tony grabbed his cell phone and stared at it for a moment, then decided against it and snapped the phone shut.

Tony tossed the phone into his console then Tony turned on the engine and flipped on his headlights. Not more than fifteen feet ahead of him stood the stringy haired man from the heroin den, leaning against the wall. As soon as the lights hit him, the man turned and ducked down the alley. Tony killed the engine and jumped out of his truck. He ran towards the alley looking for the man, but in the darkness, he could see nothing. Not only was he unable to see the man who'd run away from him, but he couldn't see the homeless men and women he'd observed before he'd entered the building. Suddenly, the darkness felt like it was surrounding him. The hair stood up on the back of his neck and he began to back out of the alley way, realizing that just because he couldn't see anyone, didn't mean that no one was there.

Tony opened the door to Harry's Tavern and was greeted with the loud noise of a full bar. The noise of music, talking, bottles, and televisions blasted Tony's senses. Pausing momentarily, Tony decided to go in anyway. Making his way through the crowded room, Tony got lucky, coming upon a booth as two young women were just leaving. Without waiting for the waitress to clear the table, Tony slid in, smiling politely at the exiting women. Leaning his back against the wooden wall, Tony stared over the large crowd. Judging from the activity, he would say there were about fifty people drinking and having a good time. Tony noted a large group of suited men and business-attired women celebrating something. There was a time when Tony would have reveled in this atmosphere after he had put an important story to bed. It was a time that made him feel alive. The chase was done, the story written, and the judgment would not come until the next day. It was those few hours that gnawed at him like a child waiting for Christmas morning to open presents. The waiting always ate at Tony. He couldn't help it. The waiting was the most painful part. With each passing minute ticking away slower than the last Tony was convinced that this waiting ate at his soul just as it was doing now.

"Can I get you something? It's Tony, right?"

Tony looked up from his thoughts and saw Sally smiling at him waiting to take his order.

Tony nodded and replied, "Seven and Seven please."

A few minutes later Sally returned with the drink and kept them coming every time she was signaled for another. The pressure was beginning to take its toll on Tony. With each passing Seven and Seven the pain didn't get any better. Tony stared into the bar, lost in his thoughts of his daughter. What was she feeling right now? Was she ok? Was she hurt? Were the kidnappers dead serious about hurting or killing her or was this some sick and twisted ploy for the amusement of some demented serial killer? Each passing image in Tony's mind was worse than the last. Like a knife being dug into his flesh, his pain grew with each drink and memory of happier times. The realization of never seeing Nicki again consumed Tony's thoughts as streams of tears uncontrollably rolled down his face. Tony buried his face into his hands, hiding his shame. The noise from the bar overpowered Tony's senses, and he could not block it out. The noise grew louder and louder, invading his thoughts. The systematic chaos made each image of Nicki harder and harder to see in his mind's eye. All he wanted was his daughter back in his arms and his wife back in his life. Tony needed his family and was lost without it. Tony was lost in his own world when he felt a hand touch his hand.

"Tony?"

Startled, Tony looked up from behind his hands and saw Sally softly smiling at him.

"Tony, its closing time. Are you ok? Do you need anything?" Sally asked looking over Tony's tear stained face.

Tony rubbed his face dry, embarrassed by his appearance, and replied, "No, No, I'm fine. Thank you."

"Do you need a cab?"

"No, I'm fine. It was just—just a bad day, I guess."

"Do you want to talk about it?" Sally asked politely, sliding into the booth opposite of Tony.

Tony looked around. The bar was empty, except for Sally and a busboy he didn't recognize. The bus boy was busy putting the chairs up on the table while attending to the cleaning of the bar and eating areas.

Turning his attention back to Sally, Tony replied, "No, thank you. I'm fine."

Tony straightened himself up in the booth, reached for his wallet, pulled out a pair of twenty dollar bills, and put them on the table.

"How much do I owe you?"

Sally put her hand over Tony's, holding it firmly.

"I mean it. If you need anything, I'm a great listener. I'm a bartender; it is kinda of my job." Sally said smiling trying to lighten the mood.

"Thank you, but no, I'm ok." Tony said handing Sally the money.

"It's twenty eight dollars."

"Keep the change." Tony said sliding out of the booth.

Sally stood up and gave Tony a hug. Taken back Tony was not sure what to do.

"I've seen you in here for years, and you always seemed to be very nice and friendly. I heard about the layoff from some of the other regulars. I know times can be tough, but you will find something else. I know it. Just hang in there, OK?"

Realizing she thought he was upset over his lost job, Tony was a bit relieved. Tony never was comfortable with people prying into his thoughts or affairs. That was one of many complaints Amy had of him.

"I will. Thank you Sally, good night."

Chapter 13

Tony woke to the sound of loud banging at the front door. He rolled over and checked the time on his cell phone. The white numbers announcing 5:30 am seem to glare back at him. Tony rose after another round of banging began.

"Just a minute for God's sake!" Tony yelled as he approached the front door.

"Good morning to you too." Amy said as she held up the morning edition of the San Francisco Chronicle and moved past Tony into the apartment.

"You look like shit Tony. Have you made any coffee?" asked Amy as she headed to the kitchen.

"No, I haven't made coffee! I was sleeping!" Tony retorted as he shut the front door. He pulled a chair back from the kitchen table and spread the paper out.

"The article's front and center: another headline for that asshole. Have you talked to the police yet?" Amy asked, pulling open cabinets in search of coffee.

"No, not yet." Tony responded distractedly as he scanned the paper for the article.

"My God, Tony! Why the hell not? This is our DAUGTHER you're messing with!"

"You don't think I know that? You don't think that I think about that every God damned minute? If I go to the police, he may kill her right away. I think he's even got a guy following me. I just don't want to take any chances."

"Someone's following you? Who?"

"I haven't been able to ID the guy. Tall guy with long, stringy hair wearing a green military jacket. I saw him yesterday when I was checking out a lead. Then, last night when I left the paper, he was standing in front of my truck. He disappeared down the alley and I lost him there. You haven't seen anyone like that skulking around, have you?" Tony asked.

"What? Wait—what do mean you lost him?! You went after him? What, are you trying to get yourself killed?!!! Tony, this is a POLICE matter! Just let them help us find our daughter! I couldn't take it if something happened to you, too!"

"Look, I'm alright. We ran into another dead end last night. I have a team at the paper researching some things. I need to call them and see if they've got anything. If they don't, I don't think we have much of a choice but to call the police." Tony conceded. "I guess I'd better get hopping; I need to get out to the prison this morning, too."

"Damn it, Tony! Today! Call the cops today! If you don't call the cops, I will! And you can bet I'll tell them everything. We can't wait any longer. Our daughter's life is at stake here." Amy choked.

"Amy, honey, I know. I KNOW! You have to trust me on this. I don't want anything to happen to her. Believe me, I don't. I'm doing everything I can."

"NO! No, you're not! You haven't told the cops what you know." Amy cut him off.

"What don't you understand, Amy? If he finds out that I've gone to the cops, it'll be game over! He'll have her killed immediately! Do you want that?" Tony snapped at Amy.

"Of course not!" Amy retorted.

"Then let me run down these leads. If I don't come up with something solid by noon, I promise I'll call Callcut. Can you at least give me the morning?"

"Not a minute longer!" Amy snapped, glaring at Tony.

Tony walked over to Amy and put his arms around her. Amy's first instinct was to pull away, but she quickly relented to his embrace and melted into his arms. Tony kissed the top of her head and held her close.

"I'll get her back. I swear that to you, honey. We won't lose her." Tony committed as Amy wept.

"Hey! Wake your fat ass up." Dante said, kicking Fat J in the ribs just hard enough to wake him. Fat J struggled to wake up, and Dante kicked him again.

"I said wake up."

"Damn man, I'm up. Quit kicking me."

Fat J rolled off the makeshift mattress on the floor and tossed the ratted old blanket against the wall. He stretched his arms, trying to shake the sleep off, he scanned the room.

"You get some coffee? Donuts?" Fat J asked.

"What? Do I look like fucking McDonald's to you? Like you need another donut. No, I didn't get a coffee for you." Dante chided, clearly angry with Fat J.

"What's up with you? What the hell did I do?"

"Did he show?" Dante asked.

"The dad? Yeah, he showed; late in the day, he showed. You should've seen it! Gypsy, that fat ho that works MLK, was rolling up on him, wanting to know if he needed a date. You should have seen his face. Man that shit was priceless!" Fat J laughed, recalling the exchange between the two.

Dante slapped Fat J hard, breaking him out of his stroll down memory lane.

"Focus! Did he get the shit?" Dante demanded.

"Yeah, yeah, he got the box. He went back over to the paper afterwards, too. Was there till I left—sometime late." Fat J said, rubbing his cheek where Dante had hit him.

"Were you followed?"

"Naw, I didn't see anyone. How'd it go here?"

"It was quiet, just me and the missus. She was stubborn for a bit, but after a while, she was just like all bitches. Once she figured out who's boss, she gave it up." Dante said with a sly smile.

"Gave up what? What the hell did you do, Deuce? You know that girl is only like thirteen right? That's like my sister, man. What's wrong with you?" Fat J scowled.

"Shut it, J! Look—I gotta check on something. You stay here with her. Watch the lots. Call me if anything moves down there." Dante said, sliding on his jacket, now securing the Glock in his shoulder holster. He glanced back over his shoulder at Fat J and shook his head as he headed down the stairs.

Nicole sat motionless in her chair, still bound by duct tape. While the chair faced the wall, her head hung limply on her chest. Fat J called out to her as he approached her from behind.

"Yo! Hey girl, you hungry? Need to take a piss? Need anything?"

Fat J spun her chair around and looked in horror at Nicole's face. Bruised and battered, her left eye was swollen shut and a cut over her right eye had bled down into her eyelid and lashes. Blood had dried under her nose but not before spilling across her lips and chin, streaking the front of her white shirt. Her left arm had been slashed three times with a blade and her right hand was swollen and bruised. He couldn't tell is the hand was broken or not. Her jeans were wet and she reeked of urine.

"Oh my God! What the hell is wrong with you Deuce?" Fat J exclaimed as he searched frantically to find Nicki's pulse.

"So, what do you want to talk about today, Ramirez?" Tony asked as he entered the interview room. "How you were just a misunderstood psychopath? You should have just gone on Dr. Phil instead of killing all those people. You'd have had thousands of Twitter fans."

Tony tossed his jacket over the back of the chair and clicked on his tape recorder, slamming it down on the table with obvious annoyance.

"What's a Twitter?" the prisoner asked, confused.

"Where the hell is my daughter Ramirez?" Tony demanded.

Ramirez sat quietly, staring at Tony. It was crystal clear who had the answers here.

Several hours later Tony made his way downtown to meet Bobby. Tony had been coming to The Espresso Depot in Union Square at least once a week for the better part of five years. It was a spot with which he was completely familiar and that he found comforting due to its bank of wide open windows, flood of natural light and high foot traffic.

Tony entered the shop, backpack slung over his shoulder, and looked around for Bobby. Across from the pastry counter, Bobby sat munching a scone at a small table. Tony slid into the seat opposite Bobby, his back to the counter so he could keep an eye on everyone coming in and heading out of the shop. Tony gave the crowd a once-over but didn't notice anything significant. Tony grabbed the cassette recorder from his backpack, popped out the tape, and tossed his recorder back in the backpack. Cupping his coffee with both hands, Bobby looked as if he hadn't slept all night and might have been wearing the clothes he'd had on the day before.

"Hey, did you get any sleep last night?" Tony asked as he slid the microcassette across the table to Bobby.

"Not much. I took a short catnap, but otherwise no. You want a coffee?" Bobby asked, picking up the tape and pocketing it.

"Did you guys come up with anything on the photos?"

"No, not really. We think the warehouse is in the South Bay, but we can't be sure. Harvey thinks the sign says "Westfield". We looked but didn't see any Westfield warehouses in the South Bay."

"We need to check it out! How many warehouses can there be?"

"A few hundred—probably more. Tony, look... you need to call the cops. We just don't have the skills or manpower for this."

Tony glared at Bobby then looked out the window.

Cautiously, Bobby asked, "What'd you get from Ramirez today?"

"Today's rant of a desperate asshole? He rambled on about this last kill: the Oakland crack house murder. He claimed that he was there to help his cousin and it got out of hand."

"Well, that's strange. There was no record of anyone else being there other than Ramirez, the women and their pimp, who he shot and killed. He said there was someone else there? We have records on where that murder took place and we have lots of records about the trial to pull from, and I have a source in SFPD that may be able to pull the case files and give me something. The case is closed, and he is going to die for the crime, so it shouldn't be all that difficult to get records from the cops. I'll check to see if they have anything else about this cousin. But Tony, I mean it: you need to get the police involved."

As Bobby focused on what police involvement could offer, Tony's attention moved to the crowd and as he scanned, he recognized a familiar face. The stringy long-haired man was sitting at the coffee bar near the back of the store. Tony noticed that the man wasn't drinking anything, but was just flipping through a local newspaper. Tony didn't take his eyes off him, waiting for the man to look up and meet his gaze. The long-haired man, dressed in a San Francisco Giants ball cap, the same green military jacket, and blue jeans continued to ignore Tony.

"Tone! Hello, are you listening to me?" Bobby asked, clearly taking offense at being ignored.

"Yeah, cops, I got it. Slowly look over your left shoulder. There's a man: long hair, Giants ball cap, in the back. This dude's been following me." Tony noted, eyes still fixed on the man.

"Seriously? You think it might be one of Ramirez's men?" Bobby asked as he slowly turned around to look then turned back to Tony.

"I don't know. Maybe, yeah. I saw him at the dope den yesterday. And when I left you guys at the paper last night, he was out near my truck. When I turned my headlights on, he took off down alley, and I lost him. Now, he shows up here. You think that's some kind of coincidence?"

"Highly doubtful. What do you want to do?"

"I'm leaving. Keep an eye on me, and if he follows me out, text me. Listen to the tape, and get me anything you can. Also, if the team comes up with anything on the warehouse let me know. I'm heading out that way. Catch you later." Tony said as he stood and slung his backpack over his shoulder.

Tony walked slowly through the shop, trying not to look like he was in a hurry. He exited through the glass doors and turned right to ensure that he'd pass right in front the long-haired man. Tony tried to walk casually as he continued north on Powell and made it two blocks before his cell phone vibrated in his pants pocket. He flipped open his phone and read the newest text, "*He's behind you.*" Tony quickly returned the text to Bobby, "*Call 911.*"

At the next corner, Tony crossed the street and turned west on Bush. Tony picked up his pace and as he passed newly polished store windows, he noticed the reflection of the long-haired man not so far behind him. Tony turned south on Mason then ducked into a beauty salon. Tony closed the doors behind him and flattened himself against the wall next to the large pane window, looking over his shoulder for the man to make the turn around the corner. Tony's heart was pumping hard sweat ran off his brow. Before Tony could lower his heart rate, the long-haired man in the Giants ball cap turned the corner and paused just outside the door, scanning the street, looking for Tony. The sound of his heart beat filled his head as Tony waited for the man to walk past the store.

"*Who is this guy?*" Tony wondered. "*If he's one of Ramirez's men, he may know where Nicki is. I should be following him, not the other way around!*"

Tony watched intently as the long-haired man passed by the salon door and continued down the block, slower than before, clearly looking for Tony among the parked cars and people walking up and down the streets. Tony turned his attention back to the interior of the salon and became keenly aware of the twenty-something eyes now staring at him. Staff and clients alike remained motionless, waiting for Tony to explain himself. Tony smiled weakly at the ladies, then looked back over his shoulder out the window but didn't see the long-haired man. He ignored the women awaiting explanation and turned away from the wall to get a better view down the block. He still couldn't see the man. Tony turned back around again and moved towards the door when the long-haired man burst in, face-to-face with Tony. The two men froze, staring at each other like children getting caught sneaking candy late at night.

Tony, who hadn't been in a fight since he was in the seventh grade, let all the rage and anger of the last few days consume him and exploded at the long-haired man. Tony rushed at him, throwing his shoulder into the man's stomach, lifting him off his feet, and driving him back out of the store, across the sidewalk until the long-haired man's back collided with a parked car. Before Tony could advance again on the man, the long-haired man took his right elbow and drove it down into the back of Tony's neck. Dizzy, Tony released him and the man shot forward with a knee to Tony's chest. Tony collapsed to the ground, struggling to get air into his lungs. Tony clutched his chest, and looked up at the man standing over him. Tony watched as the man reached into his jacket.

"Shit!" Tony yelled, but fear had taken over, and he couldn't move.

Before the long-haired man could draw his weapon, he was hit from behind by another man, the two careening off to the side. In shock, Tony stood up to see Bobby fighting off his attacker. Bobby threw a right haymaker towards the face of Tony's assailant. The long-haired man blocked the clumsy attack easily and countered with a punch of his own to Bobby's stomach, collapsing Bobby to the concrete. Before Tony could make a rush for the man in defense of his friend, two SFPD squad cars came screeching up to the curb, sirens blasting. Tony started to advance on the long-haired man, reaching him before the cops had even opened the doors to their squad car. The long-haired man raised his hands in surrender.

"STOP! God Damn it! I'm a COP!" screamed the long-haired man.

Dumbfounded, Tony stopped in his tracks, not really sure what he had just heard.

"Gun! That guy has a gun in his jacket!" Tony yelled at the approaching uniformed police officers.

Two officers drew their weapons and moved towards the long-haired man, as a third officer reached for Tony and pulled him back, hand on his holstered weapon.

"Wait! I'm a cop. I'm going to reach for my badge, SLOWLY." The long-haired man said as he reached his hand gingerly into his jacket, under the collar of his t-shirt, and pulled out a badge hanging from a chain around his neck.

A tan Crown Victoria with a red emergency light on the dash came sliding to a stop in front of the salon, and Agent Lorenzo Callcut jumped out of the driver's seat.

"Stand down! I'm in charge here." Callcut announced to the beat cops. "That officer is one of my men. Thank you, officers. Looks like everything is under control here."

Callcut strode over to the long-haired officer, who had offered a hand to Bobby. Callcut shook his head as he looked at Bobby, who was still in obvious pain and trying to recover from the punch to his stomach. Callcut then moved towards Tony, who was leaning against the window of the salon, trying to comprehend what had just happened in.

"Mr. Evans, what the hell are you doing? Attacking an officer?" Callcut barked, taking Tony by the arm. "I've got this officer." Callcut said, dismissing the beat cop.

"I didn't know he was a cop! He didn't say anything. I thought he was one of Ramirez's men. I thought he could lead me to Nicki!" Tony explained.

"Ramirez? Who might that be? You think someone has your daughter Mr. Evans?"

Realizing his mistake, Tony quickly tried to think of something to cover his blunder.

"Never mind. Forget it, Mr. Evans. We already know. Come on, get in the car. I'll catch you up." Callcut told Tony.

Tony picked up his backpack, slung it over his shoulder, and followed Callcut to his car.

"Sir, what about this guy? He was assaulting an officer." asked the beat cop. "You want us to take him downtown?"

"No, cut him loose. Unless you want to press charges, Officer Stevens?" asked Callcut sarcastically.

"Na—it's cool. No harm no foul." the long-haired man said as he climbed into Callcut's car.

Chapter 14

Tony had spent the better part of the morning sitting in an interview room in the San Francisco Police Departments Missing Person's division. He had told his story over and over for the last two hours. Bobby had been interviewed separately. Tony was convinced that no matter how many times he told Agent Callcut his story, the Agent just did not believe him. As the hours wore on, Tony became more and more stressed about the time was slipping away from them. Eventually Callcut left the room, leaving Tony to his thoughts. He started thinking about Nicki and Amy. He thought that he probably should have had a lawyer present, though he hadn't done anything wrong. Tony felt the walls closing in around him in sterile grey room. Tony stared into the one-way mirror, wondering who was back there watching him. Suddenly the door flew open and carrying a manila envelope in his hand, Callcut and the long-haired officer named Stevens came in. Callcut sat down opposite Tony, and Officer Stevens closed the door and leaned against it.

"Ok Mr. Evans. I get the big picture. I believe you, but I also think you're holding out on us. What else do you have?" Callcut accused.

"I told you everything. What do you mean?"

"Pictures. Do you have some pictures?" Stevens asked.

"Yes, in my backpack. I have two of them." Tony responded, pulling his backpack off the floor and into his lap. Unzipping the small pouch, Tony dug around and pulled out the two Polaroid photos and slid them over the table to the police officers. The two men looked at the photos closely for what seemed like forever to Tony. Tony then opened the larger compartment and pulled out the tin box in which the second photo had been placed.

"Wait, I also have this box. This is what that photo came in." Tony added, pointing to the photo of Nicki in the warehouse.

"Who else came in contact with the box?" Callcut asked.

"No one that I know of—just me. Well, me and that dead woman in the heroin den I told you about."

Stevens left the room for a moment and came back with latex gloves and evidence bags. He carefully put the photos and the box in separate bags and marked them as evidence.

"I'll get these to the lab and see if we get lucky." Stevens said as he left the room.

The door closed behind him, leaving only Callcut and Tony in the room, staring at each other.

"You should have come to us as soon as they took your kid. You've put her in grave danger."

"I had no choice! Ramirez said that his men would kill her if I called the cops. They may still do that. They may be watching me. They've been planting these photos for me to find."

"They *are* watching you. We know that. Yesterday and last night this man was following you." Callcut reached into the manila envelope and tossed three five-by-seven snapshots across the table to Tony. One photo showed a large black man sitting in a black Cadillac Escalade, looking out his driver's window at something. The second one was taken from the same angle, zoomed out to see the man watching Tony as he was walking across the street in front of the drug den the day before. The last one was a green night shot of the same man in the same car in front of the San Francisco Chronicle.

"Do you recognize that man?" Callcut queried.

"No, never seen him before. Do you know who he is?" Tony asked.

"Yeah, that's Carter Jackson or Fat J to his thug friends. Appears he's taken an interest in you. The good news is that he's more like a gofer than an enforcer. His rap sheet is mostly theft, burglary, fraud, and breaking and entering: that kind of shit. I think he was keeping tabs on your whereabouts and what you have been up to. The bad news is we don't know where he is now. We have his house, or at least his last known address covered and units watching some of the men he's known to hang around to see if he shows up." Callcut reported.

"If he knows I'm here, then Nicki is screwed." Tony replied growing agitated again.

"We've reached out to the prison and the warden. All of Ramirez's communications are being monitored. They're keeping everything looking normal, but if someone reaches out to him for instructions, we'll know. He's on death watch. No one has access to him accept his lawyer and his priest. Family visits start on Saturday." Callcut reassured Tony.

"What's next?" asked Tony.

"You need to be with your wife. We'll dust the photos and box and see if we get any hits. If Fat J pops his head up, our men will call in. We'll follow and see if he leads us to your daughter. Besides don't you have a story to write?"

"You'll tell me the moment anything happens?" Tony asked, standing up.

"Yeah, here's my card in case you need to get a hold of me, day or night. Listen, I have half the SFPD working on this. You guys keep the stories in the paper and act like everything is the same. We'll be watching for any screw up on their part. If we get a break, we'll jump on it."

Carter Jackson sat on an empty crate perched at the window sill overlooking the parking lot below. Dark clouds moved in over the city by the bay late in the morning and started to drop a steady, light rain to the area. Fat J had always hated the rain and many times wished he had the means to move south, maybe to Los Angeles to get away from the bleak weather. San Francisco got a lot of rain every year. His cousin lived in Seattle, Washington where the rain seemed constant—at least they didn't have that much, but it was still too much for his taste.

Looking down, Fat J saw Dante walking quickly across the lot and out of view, followed by the sound of the sliding door opening then being closed and locked. Fat J stood up and moved over to the top of the stairs as Dante appeared, hands on his jacket, trying to shake off the rain. Dante looked at Fat J as Fat J stood in front of him, impeding his path and staring at him. Dante pushed past his partner and scanned the loft and saw Nicole out of her chair's binding and lying down on a mattress with only her hands bound in front of her chest and the bandana gag wrapped around her mouth, sleeping. Dante stopped in his tracks and looked over at Fat J.

"What the FUCK is this? Why is that bitch out of her chair?" Dante demanded to know.

"Man, that bitch is a GIRL! She pissed herself man. And you fucked up her hands and face. What the hell is wrong with you? We are supposed to hold her, not torture her!" Fat J yelled at Dante.

"Fat boy, you better check your tone with me!" Dante said threateningly, squaring his body to Fat J's.

The two men stood nose-to-nose, staring each other down. Nicole rolled over, awakened by the shouting, and saw the two men threatening each other just a few feet from where she lay. She began to slither towards the wall.

"You just can't go and beat a kid. She did nothing to you! We all know you're stronger than her. What you trying to prove?"

"Prove? What you suggesting, I beat on something bigger? How bout I just beat your fat ass? Would that make you happy? If you don't step down, I'll just take her punishment out on you, fat boy."

"Fuck you, Deuce. I'm fucking tired of your bullshit!"

"Then make your move, fat ass." Dante said coldly, daring Fat J to act.

Fat J, before he could think it through, lashed out with a right haymaker towards Dante's head. Dante, anticipating the punch, easily blocked it with his left and quickly shuffled in close to Fat J, throwing a right elbow that crushed Fat J's nose in an explosion of blood. Dante followed that strike with a back elbow strike, finding Fat J's cheek. Two more quick strikes found the broken nose and busted open Fat J's lip. Fat J collapsed to his knees. With Fat' J's right arm still trapped beneath his left, Dante shifted his weight back and exploded a right knee strike into Fat J's battered face. Dante let go of the arm, sending Fat J flat on his back, holding his bloodied face. Before Fat J knew what was happening, the fight was over. Fat J rolled around on his back, moaning through the sound of gurgling blood.

"Don't you EVER fucking step to me, fat ass. Quit moaning like a bitch. If you ever try to challenge me again, I will fucking end you! Don't you ever question me, or tell me what to do. I will beat whoever, fuck whoever, and kill whoever I feel like. Are we clear?" Dante yelled down at Fat J.

Fat J responded in a series of groans. Dante looked over and saw Nicole trying to make her way to the stairway.

"Ah no you don't, sweet pants! Where do you think you are going? What? You don't you like it here?" Dante asked Nicole sarcastically, grabbing her by the back of her shirt and pulling back up the stairs.

Dante picked up Nicole as she kicked and tried to head-butt her kidnapper. He carried her over to her chair and, using his foot, spun the chair around to face him and slammed the young girl into the chair. Dante slammed his left hand up against the young girl's throat, pushing her up against the back of the chair, and cocked his right hand back as he prepared to punch his young victim.

"You move and I will pound your face till your eyes fall out of their sockets! Do you understand?" Dante threatened Nicole.

She stared into his eyes with frozen fear, all of her bravado rushing out of her veins. She nodded, without daring to breathe. Dante bound her hands to the chair and turned to his partner. Fat J was standing by the stairwell, using his sleeve to wipe the blood off his face and nose. Fat J turned to Dante, holding his nose.

"Damn, you broke my nose." Fat J complained.

"Shut up, you fucking baby. Here, hold still." Dante said as he took Fat J's nose between his thumbs, and set it with one swift crack.

"MOTHERFUCKER!" Fat J screamed as he wrenched away from Dante.

"Jesus man, you'll live. Get out of my face. Go get some gauze and clean yourself up." instructed Dante as he turned his back to Fat J and sat down at his perch in front of the window and looked out over the parking lot.

Chapter 15

"How long have those cops been sitting there? Tony asked Amy as he looked out the front window of Amy's parents' house.

Amy put her arms around Tony's neck and looked over his shoulder out the window at the unmarked squad car sitting in front of the her parent's house.

"They've been there since last night. Still raining huh?"

"This waiting sucks! When will your parents be back?"

"Probably a few hours. They needed to get out of the house. You told the police everything right, Tony?"

"Yeah. Callcut said his guys were going over the photos and everything Bobby and I told them. They have a lead on someone that they think is one of Ramirez's men. Ugh—I need to lie down." Tony groaned as he turned away from the window.

Amy followed Tony up the stairs and into her old room. Amy's parents still had a lot of Amy's old things in the room but had converted it to a guest room years ago. Tony pulled his cell from his pocket, opened it checking for messages, then quickly closed it and tossed it onto the nightstand and sat down on the edge of the bed.

"Any calls?" Amy asked as she entered in the room.

"No."

Amy walked around to the other side of the bed and crawled up behind Tony. She put her arms around him and pulled him close to her. Tony closed his eyes and enjoyed the calmness of her touch and the smell of her perfume.

"Lie down." Amy whispered.

Tony lay back against the soft pillows, pulling Amy close to him. She put her head on his chest and listened to his heart. Tony slowly stroked Amy's hair. Any time Amy had a hard day at work or was stressed, she had always loved how Tony knew just how to make her feel better. Over the years, Amy looked forward to the times she and Tony would lay in bed. At the end of the marriage, she had struggled with the chasm that grown between them, but times like this reminded her of what she once had with him. She missed the intimacy that needed no words. Amy raised up and propped herself up on her elbow and stared deep into Tony's eyes. Tony looked at her intently and lightly moved her hair out her face and over her ear. Amy moved her head and softly kissed his hand. Tony moved his thumb along her cheek line as she closed her eyes.

Tony pulled her close and kissed her soft lips. She let her eyes close and kissed him back, harder and more passionately. Her lips parted his and their tongues met. Tony rolled Amy onto her back, sliding his body next to her. He guided his hand under her shirt and cupped her breast. His fingers slipped inside her bra, and he gently pinched her nipple. Amy's breathing became rapid and heavy to his touch and she pulled him closer to her. Tony and Amy's emotions flowed through their bodies in a new, yet familiar, way. Time slipped away from them as they explored. After Tony finished making love to Amy with the passion of people half their age, he collapsed in Amy's arms and drifted to sleep. For the first time in close to a week, deep sleep found Tony and he embraced it.

Fat J was still checking his nose for blood as he walked to the front of his apartment complex. Fuming at how easily Dante beat him down, he made his way towards his apartment to get much needed medical supplies. Fat J thought he was careful parking his car two blocks away from his complex and sneaking up to his apartment. Lost in his thoughts, he didn't notice that the front stoop was absent of the usual suspects. Most days, the area in front of the building was littered with homies drinking beer, smoking, buying weed, and checking out young black women walking by. This afternoon the place was a ghost town.

"What the hell is this? Where are all my homies? If there is no one out that can only mean..." Thought Fat J.

"POLICE! Hands up! Get on your face Carter!!" A voice behind Fat J shouted.

Before Fat J knew what was happening four officers in blue SFPD wind breakers converged on him, guns drawn. Fat J put his hands behind the back of his head, fingers locked, and dropped to his knees.

"You know the drill fat boy. Where is she?" Demanded Officer Steven, holstering his weapon and putting Fat J into cuffs.

"Who?" Fat J asked, playing innocent.

"Read him his rights and book his ass." Stevens told one of his fellow officers. He pulled a police radio from his utility belt and walked away from the team.

"Callcut? Yeah, it's me. Guess who just showed up at his apartment? We're bringing him in."

The interrogation room door opened to the observation room. Tony and a uniformed officer entered the room. Two unfamiliar suits leaned against the wall watching the interrogation. They didn't move a muscle between them when Tony and the officer entered the room. Officer Stevens waved in Tony and gestured to the chair next to him. Tony sat and leaned over to the long-haired man, ready to ask him a question. Stevens put his index finger to his lips and gently nodded his head towards the suits. Tony took the hint and faced forward, noticing Fat J for the first time. Callcut and Fat J could be heard in the booth through a speaker box in the upper left-hand corner of the room. Fat J was trying his best to stare dead ahead at his own reflection in order to avoid eye contact with Callcut. Callcut was thundering away at his prisoner, yelling, then calming, only to explode again, trying to keep Fat J off balance. Fat J had been arrested before, so he knew the drill, and tried his best to keep it together.

Screamed Callcut, "Where the hell is she, Carter?"

"Man, like I told you and that other cop, I don't know what the hell you are talking about." "Really? No idea huh? That's not what this says." Callcut countered, tossing a manila folder on the metal desk between them.

"Shit, then maybe you need to ask that folder." Fat J cracked.

"Was it smart ass comments like that that got your face all busted up?"

"Fuck you man! You don't know shit."

"Then give me the 411! I pulled your jacket fat ass. Your sheet is full of stupid shit: B&E, fraud, and some vandalism. Kidnapping and violence is not your M.O. You want to go up for kidnapping and false imprisonment? If you don't tell me what the hell I want to know, you're looking at 20 years. Not that 1-3, out in 6 months shit you're used to. Twenty long hard motherfucking years! That's a long time with no Twinkies my man. I'll make sure your cell mate is the same asshole that you worked over at some point. You two will have plenty of time to work out all of your differences."

Fat J put his head in his hands, running his fingers though his hair, swearing under his breath, trying to process what twenty years in the pen would mean. After a few minutes, Fat J looked up at the officer.

"What'll you give me? You know—if I help you? You need to protect me." Fat J pleaded.

"Depends on what you give me, Carter. We get the girl and she's unharmed, I'll make sure to put in the good word with the prosecutor and let him know you helped us break the case. You screw me, and I'll make sure the only sun you'll ever see is through bars."

"I want that shit in writing. I help you, you help me. Man, I can't do 20. It wasn't supposed to be like this man." Fat J said, starting to whimper.

Callcut looked back at the mirror, stood up from his chair, and left the room. The suits looked at one another and left the booth without a word. Tony stared at Fat J as the big man's muffled sobs filled the observation booth. Tony's anxiety started to ramp up as time passed. The idea that the very key to his daughter's whereabouts sat right through the one-way mirror ate at him. *"What the hell were they doing cutting a deal for this asshole while his daughter's life remained in the balance???"* Before Tony could voice his complaints, the interview room door opened and Callcut stormed in and loomed across the table, causing Fat J to cower in his chair. Fat J looked up at Callcut wiping away tears with his sleeve.

"Deal. Now talk. Where is she?"

The parking lot and the street around the Baxter and Son's warehouse on Armstrong Avenue were quiet in the mid-afternoon. On the other side of Hawes, there was a series of businesses that catered to shipping and cargo and while they were usually busy at this time of day, the Baxter and Son's building had been dormant close to seven years. Largely abandoned, the semi-empty lot housed an inventory of old delivery trucks that carried the Baxter and Son's logo and miscellaneous rusted equipment. The sprawling main building was weathered and unkempt. Its blue paint was chipping from the structure beams and there was broken glass scattered along the cracked concrete from rows of broken windows. The only activity this building saw on a daily basis was the large group of workers that got on and off at the bus stop in front of it.

Dante had watched this traffic pattern every hour from 5am to 6pm for the last three days. Like ants, the workers got off and followed the pack across Hawes Street for work. Starting at

3pm, the ants streamed the other direction, back onto the bus and into their pathetically boring lives. Dante had spent many hours just wondering why the hell these people stayed in their monotonous mind-numbing daily jobs. As far as Dante was concerned, nothing could be more meaningless than punching a clock in a factory.

The first group of worker ants filled the bus to take them home, leaving the Baxter and Son's building quiet, except for the occasional seagull flying overhead. The silence was broken by the sound of police cars, unmarked and patrol cars, along with a SWAT van pealing down Armstrong Avenue from both directions. Police units cut across Hawes and around to the back of the lot while a helicopter circled overhead. Stevens' unmarked car came sliding to a stop as he slammed the cruiser into park and jumped out of the car with Callcut. Tony, in the back of the squad car, was trapped inside the cage.

"You stay here till we clear the area!" Callcut shouted at Tony as he slammed his door and ran from the car.

Police and SWAT units lined up around the Baxter and Son's building's entry points, guns drawn and waiting for the go. The air unit circled above, watching the operation unfold. When the call to go came over the radio, the team breeched the doors leading into the downstairs area, lighting it up with a flash bag. The initial unit was immediately followed by a steady stream of SWAT and SFPD officers. The SWAT made a beeline for the stairwell, sending flash bags up onto the second floor then stormed the landing. Callcut followed close behind the SWAT team as they cleared the top floor. The radios crackled to life with the "all clear" from the assigned leads. No one was in the building.

"No one touch anything! Get forensics in here; I need this place processed immediately. All information channels through me! Air one, you got anything?" Callcut barked into his radio visibly angry.

"No movement from your area. All is quiet."

"Damn it!"

Stevens and Tony joined Callcut upstairs where the Agent was studying the chair with the torn duct tape on the arms. He squatted down and looked around the base of the chair as he put on latex gloves.

"What you got?" Stevens asked as he walked up behind Callcut.

"Let's get this chair and tape dusted. May be the best chance we have for prints. Look at the tape. It looks like it was recently cut and torn at—someone was in a hurry."

"Callcut! Over here!" Yelled Tony.

Callcut warned Tony as he walked over, "What is it? Don't touch a damn thing Evans!"

Tony was standing over a mattress. A dirty blanket lay in a heap in the center of the mattress. Empty water bottles, plastic cups, and soda cans littered the floor around the head of the mattress.

"There's still steam coming out of that coffee cup!" Tony said excitedly, as he pointed to a styrofoam cup in the corner.

Callcut grabbed his radio and instructed, "Fan out! Teams check nearby cars and get some units across the street at Hawes. Expand the search radius to 10 blocks. Our targets were just here, they may still be in the area. Go find 'em!"

Chapter 16

"Did you get her? Am I free to go?" Fat J asked as he entered interview room A. From the other side of the table, Callcut stared at him coldly.

"No—we didn't get her. Looks like we just missed them. Why would Dante move her? Did you two have a back-up plan?" Callcut asked.

"Whoa! What do you mean you didn't pick them up? You didn't get the girl? Deuce is still free? SHIT! I'm a dead man! He's gonna know that I'm the snitch!"

"Slow down, fat boy. Deuce doesn't know shit. Did you call anyone? Anyone come see you?"

"No! I've been HERE, man! Just chilling in my cell. I didn't talk to no one. I swear. No one knows I'm here."

"Good. Now, tell me why Deuce would move the girl."

"Hell if I know man. That wasn't part of the plan."

"What WAS the plan? Tomorrow's Friday. What are you supposed to do with the girl? How does Ramirez get in contact with you?" Callcut pressed.

"Plan? I don't even know the plan! That was all Deuce. He told me I was supposed to come with him and just drive. That's it. When he grabbed the girl, I was supposed to keep a look out. He told me that we were supposed to just babysit her. Deuce said her father was writing about Ramirez so everyone would remember him. We're supposed to cut her loose on Saturday night. If there were no newspaper stories, then Deuce said he'd take care of it. He didn't say nothing about killing her."

"You didn't think to ask?" Callcut asked incredulously.

"Nobody tells me shit. I was supposed to get food and help babysit her. We kept watch and slept in shifts. As far as I know, no one was supposed to get hurt. Then Deuce just lost it. That dude is fucking crazy! He just kept beating on that girl. That shit ain't right. When I tried to stop him, he did this shit to me!" said Fat J, pointing to his face. "What do you think he is going to do now?"

"I don't know, but we'll find out soon." Callcut said as he stood.

"What? Whoa, wait a minute? What do you mean? I'm free to go?"

"Yep. Can't hold you anymore without anything to charge you with. You need to get up out of here before Deuce gets wind you've been here. Someone will come get you in a few minutes and process you out." promised Callcut as he left the room.

The observation booth door opened, and Callcut walked in and closed the door behind him. Tony and Stevens were already in the room.

"Stevens, reach out to the warden at San Quentin. We need to shut down all communications to Ramirez. I don't know how he's calling the shots on this, but it's got to stop!" Callcut ordered.

"His time is winding down. Family, lawyer and priest are pretty much it by now. What do you want me to tell the Warden?" Stevens asked.

"Update him on the situation. I'll bet Deuce finds fat ass soon. Let's try to buy a day. Their plan has been disrupted. I bet he will try to make contact for orders on the girl. We need to delay that the best we can."

"Right I'm on it." Stevens said as he left the room.

"What the hell are you doing letting that asshole leave? What do you mean you can't charge him with anything?" Tony demanded.

"Relax Mr. Evans. We're not going to get anything more from him. He doesn't know anything. He's just low-life pond scum. Deuce probably kept him in the dark. He was stupid enough to go back to his pad for us to pick him up, so he will be stupid enough for Deuce to find. We'll tail him, and let that happen. Hopefully Deuce will take us back to where the girl is. Then we'll book both their asses."

"That's taking a big chance with our one lead, isn't it? What if your men lose him?"

"We're not going to lose him. We'll have roving teams on him." Callcut insisted.

"You're gambling with my daughter's life!" Tony screamed.

"What DO WE HAVE? What do we have now, Mr. Evans? A fat ass kid that doesn't know shit! He doesn't know where they went. We have no leads. If he doesn't show up on the street, then this Deuce will know for sure that he was the leak, and if he is as unstable as Fat J says, then he may harm your kid. Is that what you want? We can keep him here, but what good does that do us?"

"Her time is just running out!"

"Listen, Mr. Evans. I get it. I do. I have three kids myself. And if I was in your position, I'd want to kill that bastard, too. But you need to trust me. This is not some made-for-TV movie. We're professionals. We know what we're doing. We do this all the time. If Deuce finds Fat J, we'll be there. Okay? Is that story ready for the papers?"

"I... I don't know. I need to check in with Bobby."

"Go. Go do that. We need to keep appearances up and let Deuce screw up. If something happens, I'll let you know."

Tony parked the Highlander in his old parking spot at the Chronicle. Entering the building just after 10 p.m., he made his way down the maze of hallways and into the reporters' bullpen, where he found Bobby packing up his stuff for the night. Bobby's bloodshot eyes and fatigued face told Tony all he needed to know. Bobby was burning out.

"It's almost over Bobby." Tony promised as he approached Bobby's cubicle.

"What? Oh hey, Tone. Just finishing up. Today was a bitch. I hope the story's good enough." Bobby fell back into his desk chair, rubbing his eyes and running his fingers through his hair.

"I'm sure it is. Is it in?"

"Yeah. Carol had to hold the run. We didn't have much to go on today. Pulled a lot of files from SFPD and our own archives about the last murder. Fluff mostly. We're even reprinting your story on the trial. Hopefully that'll appease him. How are you holding up?"

"Man, I'm running on empty. We're running out of time. The cops cut the fat guy free. They hope he'll lead them to Nicki or at least to Deuce. Man, I don't know. I feel like I need to be doing something—something for Nicki." Tony choked.

"You ARE doing something for her, Tony. You're doing everything you can to find her. We'll get them. You'll see—everything will turn out OK. I just have this feeling. It'll all work out. Just keep believing, Tony. You've got to be strong for Nicki and Amy."

"I know. I just want her back."

"Of course! We all do. Everyone's working on this story for you. We're all praying for you."

"Thanks. Go on, get out of here. Get some sleep. Do you have a copy for the story?"

"Yeah, here's the piece and some research sources for it." said Bobby as he handed off the manila folder from off his desk.

The two men exited the front of the newspaper's entrance, shook hands, and headed in different directions. Tony zipped up his jacket, turned the collar up to keep out the cold, tucked the file tightly under his arm, and put his hands into his pockets. He put his head down and walked towards his truck. He stopped, looked back, and saw Bobby climbing into his car. He watched as Bobby turned the engine over, and pulled away. Tony finished his short walk to his car, but didn't notice the man sitting in the car parked across the street, watching his every move. The man took a long drag off his cigarette and blew smoke into the night air. As Tony pulled out of parking structure and turned right onto Mission Street, he didn't notice the car illuminated by his headlights. Dante watched Tony drive right on by him. He started his car, silently pulled away from the curb, and drove off in the opposite direction.

It was close to midnight when Tony pulled onto Lake Merced Boulevard, driving towards his in-laws' house. He'd been driving around the last two hours, going over everything in his head. He had a feeling about Ramirez's murdered wife. He'd been thinking about the place that he'd found the last photo of Nicki. He had an unsettling feeling that he had missed something, or that the house had some other meaning that Ramirez wanted him to see. Tony just couldn't put his finger on what it was about that house, or neighborhood, but he had that undeniable feeling that there was something important about it.

Tony drove up the road and pulled into the drive way of his in-laws' place. Getting out his truck, Tony noticed the light was on in Amy's room upstairs. He nodded to the two officers in the unmarked car across the street, but neither of the officers responded. As Tony made his way up the driveway, the front door opened, and Amy stood there, dressed in black and orange sweat pants and a San Francisco Giants sweatshirt. Tony embraced her and kissed her softly. Together, they walked into the house and closed the door behind them.

Chapter 17

Tony woke to the sounds of Amy sobbing. Tony rolled over and checked the time on his cell. It was 6:30 a.m. He slid out of bed, taking a blanket with him, and put his arms around Amy where she stood, weeping as she stared out the window. Tony wrapped the blanket around both of them. Even with the heater on, she felt chilled to the bone. Tony could feel her shivering against his body. He moved her to the bed, and the pair sat down on the edge. Tony softly wiped the tears from her cheeks. The two sat there in silence for a few minutes, neither one knowing just what they were feeling, let alone how to express it in words. Less than a month ago, Amy moved out of their home, taking his daughter with her, and moved here temporarily. Now under the most horrendous circumstances, he was feeling closer to Amy than he had in years. It felt so good. He only hoped she felt the same way.

"We're not going to see Nicki again are we?" Amy asked soberly and started to cry again at the thought of her little girl, alone and subjected to who knows what at the hands of her kidnappers.

"What? No, no. We're going to get her back! The police are working a lead. Callcut was closing in on her location. He believes…"

"He believes that if you went to him sooner, like the when Nicki was first taken, we would have had the best shot at catching these assholes." Amy said, pulling away from Tony and staring into his eyes.

"Amy, we've been through this. It doesn't help to harp on what we did or didn't do. What's done is done. I'm sorry. I was doing what I thought was best."

"Why didn't you just do that damn story? I mean, really who would care?" Amy asked, becoming more upset.

"I didn't think he was going to take Nicki. I didn't think he could do anything. He's on death row in a maximum security prison. I thought he was just trying to scare me." Tony admitted, trying to defuse Amy's accusations.

"I have to get going. I'll check in with Callcut on the way to the prison. I swear to you Amy, we WILL get her back!"

Tony sat nervously in his chair. He'd been waiting in the interview room for nearly twenty minutes, but the guards still hadn't appeared with Ramirez. With each passing minute, Tony grew more and more concerned that something was wrong. Suddenly the electric locks disengaged, and the door opened to the familiar routine of Ramirez's arrival.

There was something different about Ramirez this morning. Guard Samson and his partner completed the chain-down procedure, double checking all the security measures, and exited the room. The door closed with a metallic boom that shook Tony to the bones, followed by the sound of the locks re-engaging.

"What the hell are you pulling, Evans?" Ramirez asked in a cold, yet controlled, tone.

"Writing your stories. Printing your murderous accomplishments. Isn't that what you wanted?"

"Then what the hell is that crap in the today's paper? Most of your story is stale. The story was old news. Not acceptable. You didn't do any work in uncovering my story."

Ramirez doesn't know Bobby is writing the stories, Tony thought. *This is a good sign.*

"I am tracking down whomever I can find Ramirez. You don't leave a lot of people around to speak with."

"You're not listening to what I'm saying then. You are running out of time, Evans."

"So are you, Ramirez." Tony reminded.

"I'm prepared to die. I look forward to it. Are you? Is your kid?" Ramirez snarled back at Tony.

"You bastard! Tell me where she is! She's just an innocent girl, damn you!"

"No one's innocent, Evans. You should know that by now. My parents. My wife. That asshole of a lover she had. That jerkoff that shot me when I was arrested. The guys locked up in here. Who's innocent? Kids? Damn man, I know killers that are younger than your kid. Give me a few days with her, and she wouldn't be innocent anymore." Ramirez jeered with a smile on his face.

"You sick fuck!" Tony snapped back.

"That may be so. But the fact of the matter is you have two days."

"I have one day. When the paper runs tomorrow, you tell me where she is."

"Ha, no. You'll need to find her. You needed all my stories to find her. Somewhere in the tapes we made is your answer. You're not looking hard enough. You're not listening. Maybe if you listened more, your wife would still be in your life."

Tony gritted his teeth and vowed silently not to let this animal get the best of him. Time was running out. He needed this interview, and he needed to get out there and look for Nicki. He couldn't let his hatred for Ramirez get in the way of that. *I need to stay focused,* Tony thought. Tony turned on his tape recorder and set it on the table between himself and Ramirez.

"Fine then, if you don't like today's story why don't you tell me about what happened that night? And what do you want for Sunday? That'll be the last time anyone ever hears your name."

"Adams, do you have eyes on the target?" Callcut's voice came over the police radio.

"Copy that." Sargent Adams responded, watching Fat J talking with two other gang bangers.

"What's your twenty?"

"Across from his apartment complex. He's been here for about an hour."

"Keep me posted if he moves. Out." Callcut signed off.

Sargent Adams and Officer Downs sat in their unmarked Crown Victoria down the street from where Fat J was talking with two other young black men. Adams, a veteran of undercover work for close to twenty years, put the radio down next to him on the driver seat, leaned back, sipped his coffee, and ran his fingers through his long greying beard. Having a wife and three sons hadn't slowed him down at all. Adams still felt a rush when chasing the bad guys. Downs was a rookie with promise, but was still finding his way as a cop. While Adams was more outgoing, Downs was more introverted and unsure of himself, but slowly opening up. Adams liked the kid and had taken him under his wing. He was grooming Downs as his replacement on the undercover unit.

"You think this guy is gonna show?" Downs asked Adams, looking down at an old mug shot of Dante Fischer.

"They always do. They can't resist it. Sometimes they make it too easy for us. But it just takes time." Adams reassured the rookie, checking the review mirror again.

Downs snapped photos from his high power camera and watched the men around Fat J. He seemed to be pretty caught up in the conversation and didn't notice the tall white man walking up behind him.

"Hey! Check it out! Is that him?" Downs asked excitedly.

"Hey fat ass, miss me?" Dante said to Fat J as he walked up behind the large man and placed his hand on Fat J's shoulder.

Fat J's companions faced Dante. The men stood there, staring at each other for about fifteen seconds before Fat J's friends backed away and left. Downs, watching through his camera lens, snapped photos of Dante along with the other men. Dante pushed Fat J forward, staying behind him on the sidewalk, turned left, and walked to his car. He opened the passenger door and shoved Fat J into the seat. Dante slid around the front of the car, jumped into the driver's seat, started the engine, and pulled away from the curb. He pulled a quick U turn and sped away from the apartment complex. Adams started the Crown Vic and pulled away from the curb in quiet pursuit.

"Agent Callcut, target one is on the move with target two. We have eyes on both targets." Downs reported into the radio.

Dante drove north on Third Street, watching his mirrors and looking for any police activity. Fat J sat rigidly in the passenger seat. With his back against the door, Fat J stared at Dante. The silence was intimidating to Fat J. Dante finally broke the silence after a few blocks.

"Where you been? You didn't come back."

"I... I went to get some stuff for my nose, but, that didn't work, I needed to get my nose set. I went to the hospital, man. When I got back, you were gone. I didn't know where you went, man." He lied.

"Hospital? What for? Did they call the cops?" Dante asked, getting suspicious.

"What? No, man! Hell no! I told the nurse it was nothing. Just playing some ball, that kinda shit."

"Hold on." said Dante as he turned the car onto Shafter Avenue.

Watching the rear view mirror, Dante saw the tan Crown Vic make the turn onto Shafter, three cars behind them. Dante turned left onto Jennings and slowed to watch the rear view. He watched as the tan car continue east on Shafter. Dante pulled back into the flow of traffic.

"What's up?" Asked Fat J looking around behind him.

"Cops."

"Damn." Fat J replied worriedly.

The two men kept quiet the rest of the ride. Dante kept changing direction every other block until they reached their destination. Pulling up to the curb in front of a small house on Quesada Avenue, he slammed the car into park, popped open the door and was climbing out before the engine had shut down. Fat J hauled himself out of the car and followed Dante up the driveway of the small, blue house equipped with a white security gate on the front door and security covers on the two front windows. Dante banged on the door impatiently then turned to scan for the Crown Vic. The door was finally opened by a pretty young voluptuous woman in her early twenties. Dressed in a belly shirt and shorts, she stared at the two men.

"Let me in bitch!" Dante ordered.

The blonde scowled at him and reluctantly opened the security door. She moved to the side as Dante shoved past her. Fat J waited for the girl to pass then followed her down the hallway. Inside the living room, the busty blonde lit a cigarette. A tall gaunt woman slept on the couch. SpongeBob Squarepants was on the old television set in the corner. A bong and a baggie of weed lay on the coffee table. Dante walked over to the sleeping woman and shoved her hard.

Dante screamed at her, "Get up! Get UP, BITCH!"

'Hey man, chill out!" The blonde said, leaning against the wall and taking a long drag off her cigarette.

"Shut up! Here." Dante said, tossing his keys to her.

"What's this?" She asked catching the keys with both hands as the cigarette dangled from her mouth.

"Get your dope fiend friend, take my car, and bounce. I don't care where—just go. I'll text you later." Dante instructed. He scanned the room for her purse. "I'll need your car. Where are your keys?"

"Dante, really? You need my ride?"

"I don't have time for this shit! Give me your keys!" Dante demanded.

"Alright, alright, already. They're on the kitchen table."

Dante disappeared from the room into the kitchen, swearing under his breath. The two women looked at Fat J.

"You two better get out of here. He's pretty pissed. Anyone else up in here?" Fat J asked.

"No, it's just us."

Dante returned to the living room with the keys in hand. "What are you still here for? I don't have all day!" Dante said, tossing the blonde's purse to her and pointing to the front door.

"Alright dammit, we're moving!" The blonde said as she caught her bag and crushed out her cigarette in an ashtray on the end table.

The pothead finished putting on her shoes and ambled towards the door. The women exited, slamming the door behind them without another word. Dante moved quickly through the house, looking in each of the rooms to ensure that they were alone and that all the curtains were shut. After completing his inspection, Dante returned to Fat J in the front room. The two men stared at one another, sizing each other up.

"The cops are onto us. What do they know?" Dante demanded.

"How the hell should I know?" Fat J snapped back.

"The cops raided the warehouse. They knew where to go, fat ass. How did they know that?"

"Hell if I know? Maybe they figured it out? I'm sure the girl's dad's been talking."

"You know that the photos are all bullshit man. Even if they analyzed those things all day long, they're not going to lead them anywhere."

"What? What do you mean?"

"Are you fucking fat *and* dense? Like I'm going to lead the cops right to me, so I can spend the rest of my life in San Quentin like Ramirez? Hell no. I shot those pictures in a different warehouse. So, I'll ask again, how the HELL did the cops know to raid the one warehouse in the whole Bay Area that we were hiding in, Carter?" Dante demanded angrily.

"I DON'T KNOW, man! Where's the girl now? We can't leave her alone!" Fat J said nervously.

"That's none of your concern. We have to clean this up, and I fucking mean right now. Her dad has someone working for him, writing the stories I think. Someone's doing research for him so he's got more time to snoop around. That wasn't the agreement. Now all bets are off."

"Whoa! Hold on, Deuce! What are you saying? We can't kill that kid! That's bullshit, man! I ain't no murderer. I can't kill a kid!"

"Again—not your concern. We need to clean up this shit and disappear. All loose ends must be managed. We have to deal with that reporter and the dad."

"Alright, alright. What do you need me to do? I can't do anything to that kid though. I'm telling you right now: I can't do her. She doesn't deserve that kinda shit. She's innocent, man!"

"What I need from you is to just fucking die!" Dante said to Fat J.

In one smooth motion, Dante pulled his Glock from his waist band and grabbed a throw pillow from the couch. He shoved the barrel of his gun against the pillow and then against Fat J's temple. Before Fat J could even react the muzzle flashed and his brains sprayed across the wall behind the couch. He was dead before his large body hit the wood floor.

"When I said, 'WE' need to clean up, I meant 'ME'. Don't you ever lie to me, you fucking piece of dog shit!" Dante barked at Fat J's lifeless form.

Dante moved to the window to check the street activity. For a few minutes, he scanned the street, looking at each parked car and every front door to see if anyone had heard the shot. Muffled but not completely silenced, the hit had been a risk. As in many ghettos, gunshots, even when heard, rarely evoked witnesses like in the movies. People in these neighborhoods came to realize that it was far better for their health to remain indoors and to mind their own business. When Dante was satisfied that no one heard anything, he suddenly spotted the Crown Vic parked next door. Dante could see two officers in the car, but couldn't tell if either was on a radio. He knew he couldn't take the chance.

Dante went to the back of the house and peered out the window into the decaying yard. Seeing no activity, he quietly slipped out the back door.

Adams and Downs watched the house. There was a lot of chatter on the police scanner drowning out the noise from the outside world. They had their windows rolled up to keep the sound inside the car.

"That's confirmed, Agent Cullcut. Both subjects are inside. Two women left in the subject's car, but the subjects have not left. There's movement from the windows." Adams reported.

"Sit tight, back up is five minutes away. When we get there, we need to take them. We can't wait since they're onto us." Callcut ordered.

"Copy that. We'll keep eyes on the targets 'till backup arrives. Over and out."

"Should I go around the back and make sure they don't leave?" Downs asked his partner.

"I just saw one of them peak again. They need a car if they're going to leave. I'll sit tight here while you head to the back. If you see anything, radio it in. Don't play hero got it, rook?"

"Yes Sir."

Downs turned to open the car door and saw Dante looming above him. Before the police officer could reach for his service weapon or even speak a word of warning, the windows exploded and shattered glass flew across the interior of the car, accompanied by a healthy dose of skull and brain matter. Dante fired three more shots in rapid succession into the police car, striking Adams in the chest and head. Adams' head exploded through the driver-side window, showering blood, brain, bone, and glass into the street. Dante reveled in his work for a moment then put his gun back in his waistband. Dante opened the garage, climbed into his girlfriend's beat-up red 2000 Chevy Cavalier, and calmly backed out of the driveway and drove off down the deserted street.

Chapter 18

Tony and Bobby sat in the truck parked outside Ramirez's ex-wife's place off of Martin Luther King Ave. Tony stared intently at the boarding-house-turned-drug den, as he'd been doing for the last hour and realized that nothing had changed.

"What are we doing here, Tony?" Bobby asked impatiently as he typed on his laptop.

Tony looked over at Bobby but didn't answer him. The cab of the truck was filled with the sound of Bobby typing. Tony silently wondered how Bobby could type so fast. Tony was a two-finger hunt and peck typist where Bobby had complete command of the keyboard, his fingers gliding over the keys in quick succession. Tony knew he had chosen the right person to help him with the stories. He knew there was no way he could have written the stories and still looked for his daughter, even if he could type as fast as Bobby.

"Seriously Tony what are we doing here?" Bobby asked again without looking up from his laptop.

"Don't you find it odd that there's no one out today?" Tony said, turning his attention back to the drug den.

"The other day there were plenty of people out. Now, after Lorenzo's men are sure that Nicki was kept at that warehouse and has been moved, there's no one here. I think she's in there. Ramirez was pretty agitated when he talked about this place. He was still so enraged at his ex-. I'd go as far as saying he's got an obsession about her—specifically what he did to her and that lover of hers. This place has special meaning for him."

"So call Lorenzo. You're not going in there are you? Do you have gun or something? Do you think if you show up and say, 'I'm here, I found you!' they're just going to hand over Nicki? This is not a game, Tone. They moved her because they don't want to be found. If they are found they'll be going to prison for a long time. If you're so sure, call the cops." urged Bobby, pausing between keystrokes.

"He doesn't see it like I see it. He said he can't waste man hours chasing down hunches. He said he's waiting to see if that fat guy's accomplice shows up. Look—I can't wait any longer! I need to know." Tony announced as he climbed out of the car.

"What? Wait!" Bobby clamored as he packed up his laptop and shoved it under the dashboard in hopes that it would still be there when he returned. Bobby jumped out of the truck and hustled across the street to catch up with Tony. Tony climbed through the hole in the fence and headed towards the door as Bobby gingerly made his way through the metal obstacle.

Quietly, both moved the length of the abandoned lot to the back of the building. Tony paused and looked to make sure no one was around. The notion seemed ridiculous to Bobby given that it was broad daylight, but went along with it, knowing that if he were in Tony's situation, he probably do the same thing. Tony reached the back door and tried the knob, only to find it locked.

"What the hell? How can a crack house be closed?" Tony asked sarcastically.

"What?"

"It's locked. Who locks a drug den? Kind of bad for business don't you think?"

"Tony, let's get out of here. Something's not right. I say get Callcut or even a beat cop out here and let them check it out. I got a bad feeling about this, man." Bobby pleaded.

Tony pressed his ear to the door, praying to hear movement inside. When there was none, Tony surrendered to Bobby's wishes and backed away from the door.

"Alright. You win. Let's get out of here." Tony said dejectedly.

"Drop me off at my place, will ya? I need to get through today's tape and get this story written. You know the board is concerned over these stories, don't you?" Bobby asked as he climbed into Tony's truck and closed the door behind him.

"I figured as much. How bad is it? What's going on?" Tony asked, putting on his seat belt and starting the engine. He looked in the rearview mirror and pulled away from the curb. Dante started his girlfriend's car and pulled away from the curb as well, following the Highlander down the street.

"I don't know how badly, but Carol is covering a lot on that. All she'd tell me is that it's touchy. Mostly they're pissed that we're getting almost the entire front page, and they're generally uncomfortable that we're memorializing a serial killer. Ever since the whole Zodiac thing back in the late sixties, they've been careful about this kind of stuff. They only agreed to it since it you were an employee, but that didn't mean they were OK with it."

"Well, this is the final article. He goes down tomorrow night. They don't have to run anything on Sunday if they don't want to. If they have an issue with it, let's just make sure they keep that in mind. This isn't a story either—It's my daughter's life."

Tony had never been one for politics. He was a reporter. He walked the beat for many years, covering many stories. He was good at his job, and every one of his editors over the years had known it. He was never promoted to a more senior role because he hadn't embraced the politics of running a paper. Ego was not in Tony's vocabulary, and he was perfectly okay with that. Tony didn't really see a difference between what Ramirez was doing to him and what senior management had done to him over the years: he'd been forced to write stories to bolster other people's egos. Tony lost himself in his thoughts until he pulled to the curb in front of Bobby's house in the thirteen-hundred block of Holloway.

"I'll let you know as soon as I'm done with today's story. If anything on the tape is useful, I'll call you." Bobby said as he climbed out of the car.

"The final murder right? And the full timeline right? Most of that stuff is in the case archives. Ramirez didn't say much new about it. It was like he was off his game today."

"What about coverage of the execution? Do you think there'll be protests, that kind of thing?" Bobby asked.

"Hell, no, we're not doing any of that! That wasn't part of the deal, and I'm not interested in participating in any more of this than I have to."

"It's news, Tony."

"If the paper sends you out there fine, but I don't want any part of it."

"Ok, I'll let you know if anything comes up." Bobby said over his shoulder as he walked to his front door.

Tony pulled away from the curb, again lost in his thoughts, failing to notice the red Chevy Cavalier parked down the street.

Tony's cell phone rang as he headed back towards his apartment. Tony dug the phone out of the center console and answered it.

"Tony! Where have you been? I've been calling you!" Amy exclaimed.

"I left my phone in the truck. What's going on? Are you alright?"

"That Agent guy..."

"Callcut."

"Yeah, he called they think they know where Nicki is! They've got a lead on the guy they think took her. It's incredible! They know where our baby is!"

"Amy, let's not get our hopes up. Let's see what they've got. Where are you?"

"I'm at my parents. Why?"

"I'm just south of your folks. I'm on my way. Stay put, I'll see you in a few minutes." Tony snapped his phone shut, turned his truck around and headed towards his in-laws' house.

"Are you serious?" Agent Callcut asked Stevens as he stepped up on the curb towards Dante's girlfriend's house.

"Yeah, the fat one's inside with a bullet in his head. The tails were also killed. We did recover Downs' camera. That's our guy, Dante Fischer a.k.a. Deuce. Looks like he picked up Fat J before he caught his tail." Stevens shared the photos as he and Lorenzo walked.

"And the girl?"

"No sign of her. If she was here, it wasn't for long."

"Dante's tying up loose ends. Put a BOLO out on him. I want every unit looking for this asshole. Murder and kidnapping! We need all eyes on this, and we need to pick up this dirt bag right now! Find out where this guy works and lives and get warrants. We need this guy yesterday!"

"What about the father?" Officer Stevens asked.

"Yeah, get someone on him. I'll call him and find out where he is. Also, alert his wife's detail and give them the heads up that Dante may show up there again. Have them move the family out of there. Bring them all in. They'll be safer at headquarters for the time being."

"On it boss!" Stevens said as he grabbed his radio to relay Callcut's orders.

CHAPTER 19

Bobby typed feverously on his laptop, Black Sabbath screaming into his ears via iPod. Although Bobby lived alone in the small house, he found comfort in his loud music. Somehow the sound drowned out the outside world. He'd tried time and again to explain it to others, but the sound of speed metal blasting in his head helped his thinking stay focused and clear. Bobby only removed his headset long enough to listen to the tape of Ramirez rambling on about how easy it was for him to meticulously kill other human beings without a second thought.

Bobby was no Pollyanna. He'd paid his dues and covered stories of rape and murder. Now, he covered sports by choice. He'd had his fill of death and tragedy. In sports, there was always a loser, but there was also a winner. Sports could be inspiring, unlike the world of crime. Even when the bad guy was caught and convicted, there was no happy ending. There was always a victim, and no matter how harsh the sentence, that never changed.

Cringing at the thought, Bobby put his iPod down on the table and reached for his tape recorder to listen to the interview one last time to make sure he had all the details down in his story. He closed his eyes as he heard first Tony's voice then that of Ramirez.

"It is Thursday, October 20, 2011. This is the third interview from death row with serial killer Reynaldo Ramirez. I've been looking

over the evidence in the murder you committed for which you were caught. Tell me about that night."

"What about it?"

"It doesn't make any sense to me."

"What doesn't make sense to you?"

"Well, first of all, there was a room full of people. Second, the victims are a pimp and four hookers. And lots of drugs were recovered. There is no record of you being a drug addict. You never said you used, and looking at your arms you don't show any signs of intravenous drug use. You didn't say much to the cops during the interviews, and you didn't take the stand in your defense for the murders."

"And mister reporter, what have you come up with?"

"You were there for someone else. There were reports that you may have known one of the hookers, a Julie Holloway. Was she a girlfriend or...? We all know what you did to your ex-wife when she cheated on you. I can't imagine that dating a hooker would be much easier. Ms. Halloway was found beaten and shot. Was that your handy work?"

"I was there for someone else, but not for some bitch. Doing my wife—that was a special one-time thing. I was there for my cousin. I didn't know any Julie or whatever that bitch's name was."

"Your cousin?"

"Yeah, my cousin."

"You mean...Dante?"

"So, you are catching on. Yeah, Dante. He was a good cousin, but in his youth, he got caught up with women and drugs."

"What'd you do?"

"Dante called me a few days before, saying he needed some help. He was strung-out and owed money to some asshole that was squeezing him. Dante didn't think he was up to dealing with this guy and wanted me to meet with him. I knew better than do go into that dump, but what can I say: Dante's family. I was a ghost to the cops. They had no idea where I was, or where I was operating. I figured I would slip into Oakland, take care of business, and disappear again. I met up with Dante and met the guy. This guy thought he was going to intimidate me? Not a chance. He was this little white guy that thought he was black, ordering those stoned women around like he owned them. I just wanted in and out. I told him how it was going to be and he didn't like my proposal. In the end, he pulled a 38 out and pointed it at Dante. That was his last mistake."

"What happened next?"

"This guy thought he was some bad ass or something. He was waving his 38 around and pointing it at me and Dante. I took it from him. I punched him a few times, and he cowered like the bitch he was. I ended him there with a few shots from his own gun. Then all hell broke loose."

"All hell broke loose? What do you mean?"

"Dante freaked out. Yelling at me, yelling at the bitches. Screaming we had to waste them because they are witnesses. These women were so stoned they had no idea what was going on. I'd just smoked their pimp and none of them paid much attention to us. Even if they did, what were they going to do? Go to the cops? Dante wouldn't listen and he pulled his Glock out and started killing those hookers. I didn't want no part of that. That's just too much noise and attention. As I was leaving out the back I got hit in the back of the leg. I got a few blocks down the street but I couldn't get the blood to stop. The cops showed up really fast. Someone had to have called them when I killed that punk ass wannabe. When the cops got to me, at first they didn't know what they had. I told them I was just passing by when something 'bit' me. At the hospital the doctors pulled a nine millimeter slug out of my leg. Didn't take the cops long to figure out who I was and where I was coming from."

"You didn't say anything about Dante? You took the heat for all those murders? You're ready to go down for crimes you didn't do? Why in the world would you stay quiet?"

"Esa es mi familia. That's what it means to be family, man. Besides what difference would it have made? If cops didn't pin *those murders on me, they'd have eventually pinned shit on me that I did do. Besides, if I have learned anything in prison, it's these two things: no one is innocent and absolutely no one gets out alive."*

Bobby put the finishing touches on the story and got ready to post it for the evening submission. He leaned back in his chair and stretched his arms and body. Bobby rose and turned around, right into Dante Fischer.

Bobby stumbled back as Dante's fist met his face with full force. Bobby staggered back and fell to the floor, his nose bleeding and his eyes watering.

"What the hell do you think you're doing? Who said *you* could write about my cousin? I don't seem to remember you being chosen for that honor!" Dante said as he walked slowly towards Bobby.

Bobby, staggering to his feet, put his hands up in front of his face, trying to appear tougher than he was. Dante laughed at his feeble attempt. Dante just shook his head and jerked toward Bobby as if he was going to punch him again. Bobby flinched at the feint and caught Dante's boot full in the chest, sending Bobby into the built-in cabinet in the wall. Bobby hit the back of his head against the wall and fell to the floor again clutching his chest, struggling for breath as jars and cans rained down on Bobby, bouncing and breaking against the ceramic floor.

"Who are you?" Bobby gasped.

"I'm the clean-up man. Hate to tell you this mister, but, "wrong place, wrong time. Your newspaper services are no longer needed." Dante aimed his Glock at Bobby's forehead. Bobby's eyes widened in horror, and the air escaped his lungs as his limbs went stiff with fear. Bobby couldn't even move his hand over his face in a weak attempt to deflect the bullet. It was the moment of death that Dante missed from his military days. It was the moment before pulling the trigger that gave his life meaning. Bobby came into this world the same way he exited it: in a flash of light that he would never remember.

Lorenzo Callcut and Officer Stevens entered the interview room. Amy and Tony, along with Amy's parents, anxiously awaited news. When the officers came in the door, the women stood up excitedly. As much as Callcut tried to hide his emotions, the family saw it instantly. Amy started to cry as her mom grabbed her and pulled Amy close.

"Nicole wasn't at the house where we thought she was being held. It doesn't mean that any harm has come to her. We had officers tailing Carter's accomplice, but he slipped away. We know who the man is, and we have a citywide alert out for him. We've also informed all state law enforcement to be looking for this man border to border, though we think he's remained local."

"He got away?" Tony said, agitated.

"For the time being, but not for long. We have every officer looking for this guy. Whatever rock this guy crawled under we'll find. I promise you that."

"Where's the other guy? Tell me you have him. Please tell me he has something to say."

"We've got the other guy, but he won't be telling us anything though."

"I don't care Agent Callcut! Make him talk! The government does it all the time! We have to make him talk!" Tony screamed.

"Tony, even the government can't make dead men talk."

The family stood there, stunned. Only the muffled sound of Amy's sobs broke the silence.

"Look, we're doing everything we can to find this guy right now. In the meantime, I have authorization to place all of you in one of our safe houses until we catch this guy. We don't know exactly what he knows, but we do know he knows where the Quinns' live. I want to make sure he doesn't have access to any of you." Callcut offered.

"I can't be on lockdown." Tony retorted.

Stevens stepped forward. "I figured as much. For the next few days, I'll be your shadow. Where you go, I go."

Tony opened his mouth to protest but caught Amy's glare at him. He knew she wanted to make sure he was safe, and if having a personal bodyguard from the SFPD made her feel better then Tony would just have to get used to it.

"What about Ramirez? What about his communication?" Tony asked finally.

"He's on lockdown, too. He is only being allowed the contact afforded him by the law as a prisoner in his final hours on death row. All phone and mail correspondence have been suspended until this is over. Only his family, lawyer and priest are allowed to see him. It's the best we can do for now. An officer will be in shortly to get you out to the safe house. If anything changes, you will be the first people I call." Callcut said as he exited the room.

Tony left his family waiting for the police escort to the safe house. He didn't like the feeling of being watched. He felt to his core that he was close to finding his daughter, and there was something about that drug den that gnawed at him. Tony climbed into his Highlander and turned into traffic and headed back to the crack house, determined to uncover its real meaning to Ramirez. Tony called Bobby several times during the drive but kept getting his voice mail. Given that Bobby had been attached to his cell since he got it, Tony was unsettled by his inability to reach Bobby. Feeling something was not right, Tony turned towards Bobby's place.

Tony parked a hundred feet down the street and walked up the sidewalk to his friend's house. Tony kept looking over his shoulder, not really sure what he was expecting to see. The sky was darkening as the sun was setting and clouds were beginning to cover the Bay Area. The forecast called for rain, and it looked like the weather man had it right this time. The heavy smell of an impending downpour was in the air.

Tony raced up to the front door, knocked, and rang the doorbell impatiently. He noticed that Bobby's car was in the driveway. Tony walked the length of the house to the gate leading into the back yard. Half running, half walking, Tony went to the back door and banged loudly on the door. Receiving no response, he tried the doorknob. The knob turned and Tony opened the door. He took this as a bad sign.

Tony entered the house, waiting for his eyes to adjust to the darkness. He searched for a light switch, but had no idea where it was located.

"Bobby? Hey Bobby, It's Tony. You here?" Tony called out into the blackness.

Sudden movement from the front room caught Tony's attention. A flash of light erupted from the direction of the sound, then Tony felt a blow to his nose and found himself reeling back, hitting his head on the kitchen table. The overhead light blasted to life, and as he held his nose with one hand, Tony raised his head to identify his assailant.

"Well, Well, Daddy. We finally meet. Feels like I know you already. Are you alone?" Dante asked, standing over Tony.

Dante was dressed in a hooded sweatshirt, a long military camouflage jacket, blue jeans, and black work boots. Tony noticed the black leather gloves the man was wearing. Dante moved to the back door, closed it softly and locked it. Tony sat motionless and kept his eyes on his attacker.

"Seems like a lot of people have been looking for me. You made it easy for me, because I was looking for you too." said Dante. He reached down and grabbed Tony by his jacket and, with amazing ease, lifted him off the floor and tossed him across the kitchen into the cabinets. Tony crashed to the floor then tried to stand up. Dante moved towards Tony as Tony staggered to his feet and lashed out a right haymaker punch, easily deflected by Dante, who followed up with an elbow to Tony's jaw, dropping Tony to the ground again.

"Your kid seems to think you're going to save her. She's severely mistaken. You fight like shit, old man. You haven't been playing by the rules have you Mr. Tony Evans?"

Dante towered over Tony. "Do you know who I am?"

"You're Dante, Ramirez's cousin. Where's my daughter? "

"Ahh… very good. You *do* know who I am. And no, I can't tell you where she is. You cheated the rules, no? Had someone else write the stories you were hired to write? You're a liar and a cheat, Mr. Evans. You didn't follow the rules, so you don't get the prize."

Tony leapt from his kneeling position and wrapped his arms around Dante's waist, shoving his shoulder into Dante's stomach, trying to drive him back. Dante easily spun Tony around, driving his elbows into Tony's shoulder blades, opening Tony's grip and sending him to the floor again. Tony looked up at Dante and caught a strong right hook to the face loosening a few teeth, and draining the fight right out of him.

"You've got spunk. I'll give you that. Now I know where your kid gets it. But I want you to know this. You're not going to find her. She'll be dealt with, like your friend there. And I want you to think about that. Your arrogance cost your kid her life, and you'll have to live with that for the rest of your life. When you think of her, think of me." Dante bent over and slugged Tony one last time, bouncing Tony's head off the ground. It was the last thing Tony saw before the lights went out.

Chapter 20

Tony woke to a massive ringing in his ears, dried blood on his face, and an aching body. Tony hadn't been in a fight since he fought Eric Dell in the fourth grade. And as Tony remembered, that fight didn't go so well either. As Tony slowly pulled his head up off the tiled floor, he noticed Bobby's body splayed out at the entrance to the hallway.

"Bobby!"

Tony moved as fast as he could, but he knew it was too late. Bobby was cold to the touch and the pool of blood by his midsection had started to coagulate. Tony stopped short of the blood pool. He fell against the wall and dug his phone out of his pocket to dial 911.

A half-hour later, the police, along with Officer Stevens, were investigating the scene of Bobby Jenkins' murder. Tony was sitting on the couch in the living room, giving his statement, holding an ice pack to his swollen face. After reviewing the events of the day, including his first-and-only encounter with Dante Fischer, Tony told the police the obvious.

"Dante knows everything, but he did say that Nicki is still alive. He can't be allowed access to Ramirez."

"He told you this?" Stevens asked suspiciously.

"Yeah, while he was kicking my ass. Man look around. Do you see a laptop or any other computers here? He had to have taken the computers with him. He knows everything. I guess that's why Bobby was killed. Damn, he's dead because of me." Tony said sadly.

"You didn't kill Bobby, Dante did." Stevens offered. "But why'd he leave you alive?"

"He wants me to live with the threat of Nicki's death. He wants to keep torturing me with that thought. I need to call the paper." Tony informed the officer, excusing himself not waiting for permission to end the interview.

Tony walked outside and closed the front door to keep the chaos of the murder scene away from him. He pulled out his phone and dialed Carol Gibson. The phone rang twice before she picked up.

"Tony! Is that you? Have you heard anything?" Carol asked.

"Please tell me you have Bobby's article for the morning edition." begged Tony.

"No, Not yet. I haven't looked yet. Hold on. Did he submit it? Let me go in my office and check my email. Did you hear anything about your daughter?"

"I know she's alive. I just ran into the kidnapper—literally. It wasn't pleasant. Are you at your computer yet?" Tony asked impatiently.

Tony could hear Carol close the door to her office, shuffle some papers on her desk, and begin typing on her computer keyboard. After a few moments, Carol came back on the line.

"Yeah, hold on—let me open the attachment. Yeah, I have it. He sent it over at 3:30pm."

"If you're with him, I'll need him to come in and sign off on the editorial copy. I'll send the story over now."

"Carol—Bobby's here but he won't be signing anything—ever—again. Carol, Bobby's dead."

Tony could hear Carol gasp on the other end of the phone and struggle to say something. After a minute of sobbing, Carol composed herself enough to ask what had happened.

"He was shot and killed in his house—sometime after he submitted the story. He wasn't answering his phone, so I came over here to check in on him. The killer was still here. It was the same guy who took Nicki."

"My God, Tony! Are you OK? Are you hurt?" Carol asked with concern.

"I'm OK. I've got some bruises and a massive headache. Listen, I need to go and give the cops a little more information. I'll be down later tonight to sign off on the copy if you don't mind."

"Tony, can you hold on for me? Someone just came in to my office." Carol said, pulling the phone away from her ear before Tony could respond.

Tony could hear muffled voices, trying to make them out, but to no avail. He could hear Carol's tone but couldn't make out what she was saying. Tony heard her office door shut again, followed by Carol's voice back on the other end of the phone line.

"Tony, I need you to come in as soon as you can. We have a problem. How soon can you get here?"

"Publisher?" Tony asked.

"Just get here as soon as you can." Carol insisted evasively.

"Give me a few minutes. Let me wrap up here with the police, and I'll be right there."

"Fine. Just hurry." Carol said, hanging up the line before Tony could respond.

An hour and a half later, Tony sat waiting in the waiting room of the executive offices at the San Francisco Chronicle. The hallways were dark at this time of night, but Tony could see the glow of light from Carol Gibson's office. As Tony arrived at the paper's office, Carol texted him to wait in the waiting room until she came for him. He let her know that he was there. Fifteen minutes later, he texted her again. He finally heard Carol's office door open and the sound of her high heels clicking down the linoleum hallway.

"Thanks for waiting, Tony. You can come in now. Are you sure you are alright? Again, I'm so sorry to hear about Bobby. I still can't believe it." Carol hugged Tony, trying not to cry again at the thought of Bobby's death. She turned away from Tony so he wouldn't see her tears and led him down the hall towards her office.

"I'm fine. I still can't get over Bobby, but Carol, what's going on?" Tony asked.

"I think it would be best it came from leadership." Carol replied without turning back to look at Tony.

"You can't be serious." Tony said with disgust, staying behind Carol as they disappeared into the darkness of the empty hallway towards the glow of her office.

It had been no secret over the years that The San Francisco Chronicle had been in deep financial trouble. The paper had had five different publishers since 1993, and had bled millions over the last decade. Multiple attempts at restructuring and reduction in staff had not held off what many experts felt was the inevitable. The underlying feeling in the hallways of the paper was that it was only a matter of time before the doors closed on the print side of the paper. Because of concerns over circulation, senior management had been more cautious than ever about what they printed. Anything too controversial was taboo as execs feared that readers might stop their subscriptions.

Carol and Tony turned the last corner of the hallway and came to Carol's office. As she opened the plain brown, wooden door, Joe Armstrong, President of the Chronicle paper and the second-in-command, stood to greet them. Executive Vice President and Editor Archie Wagner followed suit, extending his hand to greet Tony as he entered the room. Tony had never met any of the executives before. During all the years Tony had worked for the paper, these men, along with the Publisher, had always been mere names on the org chart. It was extremely rare that executives this high up the chain would call on anyone below the Editor-in-Chief. The fact that these men came calling at this late hour told Tony what they had to say was grave.

Joe Armstrong greeted Tony first, standing and shaking his hand with an iron grip. Although well into his seventies, the handshake took Tony by surprise. Dark eyes peered over silver steel-rimmed glasses to meet Tony's. He nodded his silver-haired head towards Tony as Carol introduced the men. Tony noted that Mr. Armstrong's impeccable black and grey striped suit didn't have a wrinkle in it; a polished diamond filled Rolex watch caught his eye as Mr. Armstrong pulled his hand back. Archie Wagner nodded to Tony when introduced. Mr. Wagner was much younger, and in his late fifties, and had a much weaker handshake. With his dyed hair, a vain attempt to look younger than he was, Mr. Wagner gave Tony a dry smile, then backed away, allowing Tony to make his way into the office.

Carol took her seat behind a large old, brown, wood desk. The office was bright with newly painted white walls and dark trim. Though the paper revenue and subscription base was down, the paper had tried to raise morale with little things around the office: new paint and minor maintenance to offices and common areas had been completed over the last eight months. It hadn't been expensive, but gave the office a facelift as the paper moved into a new era. Carol had decorated her office with some small, green plants and Zen gardens, along with a Newton's Cradle. Carol picked up a hot cup of tea she'd been sipping and took a long drink, watching Tony and her bosses. Mr. Wagner stepped back and leaned on the edge of a light table that glowed dimly in the corner of Carol's office. Mr. Armstrong, making sure the door was closed, leaned against the door with arms folded, wrinkling his immaculate suit.

"Mr. Evans thanks again for coming in. Please have a seat." said Mr. Armstrong as he gestured to the chair in front of Carol's desk.

Tony sat down uncomfortably and awaited Armstrong to sit in the other chair, but he remained standing against the door. Tony took this as a statement of power. After a moment of awkward silence, Tony broke the tension.

"So, what can I do for you? Why did you call me in here, Carol?" Tony asked.

"We have some...concerns over these stories we are running on your behalf, Mr. Evans." Mr. Armstrong said.

"And I have a feeling that I'm about to have some concerns too. What's going on?" Tony asked Mr. Armstrong piercingly.

"These stories you and Mr. Jenkins are running about Mr. Ramirez. We're growing increasingly uncomfortable with the content and the message being sent." inserted Mr. Wagner.

"Uncomfortable? You're uncomfortable? My daughter has been kidnapped and is being held by this guy's thugs. You're not the only one who's uncomfortable." Tony fumed at Mr. Wagner.

"The publisher's position and the policy of this paper are not to run this type of material. Giving a killer more press than he deserves just leads to other headline hounds looking to get press. Our readers don't want to read that."

"The man is condemned and due to die tomorrow night. That is news: another execution at San Quentin by the state of California. Like it or not, that's news. This guy has been in the can for close to 20 years. He has a lot of history with this city when he operated..."

"...It is the opinion of the publisher not to run any further stories." Mr. Armstrong cut-in with a deep and final tone.

"What? Why? If the story doesn't run, my daughter dies! It was my understanding that we had a deal. Run these stories until we can get my daughter back or until this guy is executed." Tony barked at Armstrong.

"The situation has changed."

"The situation hasn't changed! Nicki is still out there and not home with us! Ramirez is alive for another 24 hours or so. Nothing has changed!"

"Maybe from your point of view it hasn't but from ours, it has." Mr. Armstrong said coldly.

"What has changed?"

"We've been getting complaints—mainly from the families of Ramirez's victims. They don't want to see him memorialized any more than he already has been. These stories are dredging up their losses."

"Carol, how are the numbers trending for the online edition during the last week? How many hits is the online edition of the paper getting?" Tony asked, rising from his chair and leaning over Carol's desk.

"We've seen a steady increase in traffic over the last week, five to ten percent every day. As of this morning, our readership or hits online has been up almost twenty five percent." Carol smiled behind her teacup.

"So, your readership is up this past week, my daughter's life is on the line, and you're worried about a few complaints? Don't get me wrong, I feel for the families that Ramirez has affected, I really do. I can sympathize with them. I don't want to *become* one of them. If you pull the story, my daughter *dies*. Unfortunately, we can't do anything for those families. The state will do its best to give them peace in less than a day, but the paper not running this final article is not going to do them or my daughter any good. You can do something for my daughter. Are you willing to risk her life for a few complaints? Is that really what you want?" Tony thundered.

"You're putting the paper in a difficult position Mr. Evans." Armstrong snapped.

"No, Reynaldo Ramirez is doing that. I asked for your help and compassion, and up to this point I've been grateful. But, we have one day to go, then the Sunday edition covering this bastard's death. That's the last you will hear of Ramirez. I know you can't tell the other families about my daughter, but is the elimination of one story really worth her life?"

"These are delicate times, Mr. Evans, for the paper..." Mr. Wagner cut-in.

"You're telling me! What if this was your kid or your wife, Mr. Armstrong? Would your precious policy and procedures stand up for them? You pull that story; you may as well pull the trigger on my kid!" Tony bellowed, exasperated.

The four of them stood in silence looking at Mr. Armstrong. He leaned with his back against the door to Carol's office, folded his arms again, head down in thought. Tony flashed a look at Carol, and then glared back at Mr. Armstrong.

"The online numbers are up, Carol?" Armstrong asked, without looking up.

"Yes, sir."

"What about circulation numbers from the newsstands?" Mr. Wagner asked.

Carol turned to her computer screen and pulled her keyboard toward her. After a few mouse clicks and queries from her keyboard, she looked up at her bosses.

"Up eight percent this week." Carol reported.

"Alight Carol, run the story. I'll take care of this." Mr. Armstrong spun around, wrenched open her door and exited quickly. Mr. Wagner followed behind his boss.

"Mr. Evans, I hope you appreciate our sensitive position. I...I'm sorry for your daughter." Mr. Wagner said before turning and disappearing into the darkness of the hallway.

Tony pulled to a stop, parking his truck into an empty spot at the bottom of Taylor and Pine streets. His GPS system took him to the address that Officer Stevens had given him, pointing him to the location of the safe house that his Tony's family is staying in. Tony got out of his truck and locked it moved quickly across the street, and walked up Pine Street. Tony stared at the plain white building that stood before him: non-descript multi-unit place with a dull white finish that blended in with all the other boring colored housing units on the block. Tony looked around his surroundings, casually trying to see if anyone was watching him. Convinced no one was there; he made his way up the short stack of stairs and entered the first floor of the building through weathered wooden doors. Climbing to the second floor, Tony saw a large man in a suit sitting outside an apartment. As Tony approached, the large man stood and faced Tony, speaking softly into a radio handset in his left hand.

"It's alright, I'm Tony Evans. My family is in there by order of Agent Callcut."

"One minute please, Sir." The larger man said, repeating Tony's information into the radio.

The two stood facing each other with an uncomfortable silence surrounding them. The large man never took his eyes off of Tony. A long silent minute passed in the dimly lit hallway until the large man responded into his radio. The door to the condo opened and Tony's mother-in-law, Lindsay, poked her head out and verified that Tony was who he said he was. The large man nodded at Tony and allowed him to pass into the condo as he resumed his post on the chair just outside the door.

Tony entered the 8,000 square foot condo mesmerized by how large and well decorated the condo was well lit with track lighting, comfortably looking furniture, large LCD TV mounted on the wall, surround-sound speakers built into the walls and ceiling. A ceiling fan hummed quietly above his head. Beautiful paintings hung on the brightly colored walls.

A very large heavy-set SFPD officer carrying two cups of coffee shuffled towards Tony, wheezing loudly. He handed one of the coffees to Lindsay, as she made her way past the two men into the kitchen. Tony's father-in-law, Carl, sat quietly in the corner, reading a book.

"Confiscated drug house." the officer stated loudly.

"What?" Tony said, dumbfounded, turning his attention to the policeman.

"It was a drug house that we raided years ago. The property was seized and now belongs to the City. That was what you were thinking, right? How the police can afford something like this? They all wonder that." the large man wheezed.

"Oh, I see. Where is my wife, Amy?"

"Down the hall, on the right I think." the overweight officer said, sitting down at the kitchen table, sipping his coffee.

Tony made his way down the immaculate hallway. As beautiful as the place was, his thoughts turned to Amy and his missing daughter.

Knocking on the first bedroom door on the right, Tony heard someone moving around on the other side of the door. The door opened slightly, and Amy's face peeked around the door to see her visitor, expecting to see one of the police officers. Realizing it was Tony, she opened the door wide, smiling at him, and invited him in. Amy obviously had been crying in her solitude, dressed in a t-shirt and fuzzy pajama bottoms. With no make-up on and her hair pulled back tight, she never looked more beautiful to Tony. Tony entered the darkened room and closed the door behind him. Amy embraced Tony and melted into his arms. Tony kissed the top of her head and held her closely and silently. He felt at home again. It had been a very long time since he had felt this feeling. In Amy's arms he felt that he was safe, and it was not until this very moment that he realized that he hadn't felt like this in years. Tony missed Amy more than words could describe. Amy pulled away and looked deep into Tony's eyes, studying every line in his face. Sensing something wasn't right, Amy gave Tony a puzzled look.

"It's Bobby, Amy. Bobby's dead." Tony said softly, struggling to say the words.

"My God." Amy said softly, covering her mouth in disbelief. She turned away from Tony and sat on the edge of the bed.

Tony looked around and found a chair in the corner. He pulled the chair to the foot of the bed and sat in it, facing Amy. He took Amy's hands into his and stroked her hands and fingers softly as they sat in the darkened room quietly. Soft light from the streetlight outside poured through the window, illuminating Amy's face. Amy sobbed softly as Tony wiped her tears away from her cheek. She looked up into Tony's eyes, searching from something comforting to say. Tony took Amy's face and held in gently in his hands, leaning in to gently kiss her soft lips. One kiss was followed up by an even tenderer one. Before Tony could kiss her a third time, Amy pushed Tony back, keeping him at arm's length, and looked at him, confused and scared.

"Tony, what are we doing?" Amy asked softly.

"What do you mean?"

"You and I is what I mean. What are we doing? A week ago we were on our way to separate lives. As much as I loved being with you the other day, I can't keep just doing that."

"What do you want, Amy? Remember, you left our home." Tony said, trying to choose his words carefully.

"I want you, damn it! I want you to want to be with me, with Nicki. I want Nicki home, and I want us to be a family again. I never wanted to leave, Tony, but you gave me no choice. You left us."

"I left you? I didn't leave you." Tony pleaded.

"Yes you did, you left us mentally. It was like you didn't want to be around us. When you were there physically, you were not there mentally. I know you were not with me. You didn't touch me anymore. It was like you didn't want me there."

"I know, Amy I know. I realize that now. As horrible as this whole thing is, it puts your life in perspective. I have been doing a lot of thinking over the last few days, and I know what I want. The most important thing to me is you and Nicki. I never wanted to lose you guys. Never. I just didn't realize it until you were not there. With you and Nicki gone, I don't feel complete. I don't feel right. I just feel—hollow. I feel empty, and I don't want to feel like that anymore. I want you back, back with me, by my side and in my life." Tony cried, holding Amy's hands in his.

"When this is all over, then what? I love you. I never stopped loving you, but I don't want to feel abandoned anymore. Your work consumed you and you let it. You let it take you from us. And what about the next job? Will it be the same then too?"

"I know, and that will *not happen* again. Amy, I swear to you *that would never happen* again. I know I have done wrong with you and I know that it will not happen overnight, but I hope you give me the chance to prove it to you. I can change. I will change. I swear baby, I will change. You and Nicki is all I have and I will do everything in my power to make sure that I *never, ever* hurt you guys again. I swear to you Amy, I love you with all my heart. I just want to come home again. I want you. I love you, since the moment I saw you in New York I have loved you. That has never changed." Tony said, pouring his heart out to his wife.

Amy reached out to Tony, pulling his head to her chest as Tony sobbed, letting out days of fears and months of sorrow. Amy just rocked slowly holding Tony to her. Tony wrapped his arms around Amy's waist and held her close to him, never wanting to let her go ever again.

"I know baby, I love you too. I never stopped loving you either Tony."

Chapter 21

Saturday morning Tony made the drive out to San Quentin. The skies were dark with the impending storm that had been threatening the Bay Area for the last twelve hours. The rain had been steady since four in the morning when Tony had woken to the sound of the rain hitting his window. His eyes were heavy and his five o'clock shadow had become a three-day adventure without shaving. The gray in his beard made Tony look much older than he really was. Tony fought the urge to let his eyes shut as he made his way through the gates of the prison near the visitor parking lot. A small group of activists had started to gather in the rain under umbrellas and mobile tarps. A priest led the group of seven in a hymn. Every time there was an execution scheduled at the prison, it brought out the activists. Most of them sided with sparing the killer. Tony always found it funny that during the trial, the majority of people wanted the killer convicted, but then had a change of heart when the sentence was due to be carried out. Of the executions that Tony had covered over the years, he estimated that only ten percent of such gatherings were for the victim or victims of the crime, and those were usually family members. Something about that just never sat right with Tony. Tony pulled into a parking stall, took a copy of the day's paper off the passenger seat, stuck it into his jacket, and stepped into the rain. Jogging past a news crew from Channel 2 setting up for the morning newscast, Tony made his way towards the visitor security entrance.

Tony was just settling in when Ramirez was escorted into the room. Two different guards worked their way through the security protocol for Ramirez as he sat seething, staring at Tony. Tony took his seat just as the guards completed their final security check and left the two men. When the security bolts locked into place, Ramirez let loose on Tony.

"You motherfucker!" Ramirez screamed at Tony.

"Excuse me? What are you bitching about? I got your story printed, now give me my daughter!" Tony shouted back.

"Give her back? No chance. You broke the rules of the game. You thought you were smarter than me. You don't follow orders too well do you Mr. Evans?" Ramirez asked coldly.

"Funny, my wife says the same thing. I got your story, right here." Tony said, holding up his copy of the San Francisco Chronicle. "I got your story in the paper each day as you asked. Now give me back my daughter. Give her back, Goddamnit!"

"I said I wanted YOU to write my story, not some patsy with your name on the story."

"What are you saying?" Tony asked, coyly.

"You lie like shit. My bitch of a wife lied better than this shit when she was fucking that guy years ago. From the look of your face, I guess you met my cousin?"

Tony paused in panic for a moment, silently searching for something to say. Every lie ran though his brain at light speed. His heart started to race and sweat beaded on his forehead. In the end, he chose truth.

"Yes."

"Lawyers have a saying, Mr. Evans. Never ask a question for what you don't know the answer. I know your game. I don't blame you. You're a father. You did what you thought you had to do. You made a call. But you lose. The bitch is as good as dead. My cousin knows what to do. Your actions have killed her. As I understand it, you killed your reporter friend, too."

Ramirez leaned forward, straining his chains against the chair, smiled callously at Tony and fed off the fear and pain his words inflicted upon the reporter.

"How do you know all of this, you've been on...?" Tony asked, stunned and realizing that he might never see Nicki again.

"Communication lockdown? Please—the police can't seal up shit. How do you think gangs keep going when leaders are doing a stretch? Reporter man, everyone and everything has a price in here. All one has to do is find it. Yours was your kid. I got you to do what I wanted you to do, right? That's all this life is. What price are you willing to pay? What are you willing to do to get what you want?"

"I want my daughter!"

"No. I'm taking that bitch to the grave with me. Chock that one up as my last achievement in this world."

"I want my daughter you sick bastard!" Tony bellowed.

"What are you willing to do for her?" Ramirez said, leaning back in his chair, reveling in having the upper hand.

"What do you want?"

"That is the wrong question Mr. Evans."

"What is the price?" Tony asked, defeated.

"Mmmm you haven't figured it out yet?"

"WHAT IS THE PRICE YOU ASSHOLE?!" Tony screamed as he stood.

"I only deal in death. If YOU did the work I asked you to do, YOU would have known that by now. I ONLY deal in DEATH!" Ramirez barked back at Tony.

"You want me to die? Die for Nicki? Fine, let's do it. Let's go! I'm yours!"

"You ready to die? There are many ways to die, Mr. Evans. Being locked up in this prison, these cells, you die a little every day. You want to die for your kid? Take her place? It's a nice sentiment. If I was on the outside, I might even consider it. It's a noble sacrifice. But you're late, my friend. I can't do anything about it now, but it is good to know that you would die for her. If there were more people in the world like you, those that would make sacrifices, then maybe there would be hope for the world. If there were more people like you, then maybe I would never have ended up in this shithole."

The security door clanged to life as the bolts snapped apart and the door started to open. Ramirez looked towards the door and then back at Tony.

"I gotta go. I have a date with the state tonight. Oh and with your lovely little girl. I hear she's pretty. I'll make sure I say hi for you and let her know you would have died in her place."

'YOU SICK TWISTED BASTARD! WHERE'S NICKI?" Tony said, screaming at Ramirez, banging on the security fencing between them.

Two officers opened the visitor's door and came in behind Tony, grabbing him from behind and pulled him out of the room as Tony screamed at Ramirez in desperation. Tony pushed the officers, trying to get away and back to the fence, as close to Ramirez as he could. As Ramirez stood, his shackles clanged, his long stringy hair flowed in his face, his eyes glared and with a slight smile he was led into the row.

"NOOOOO! Where is SHE?" Tony screamed, and fell to his knees as he heard the security bolts lock into place, isolating him from the one person that could give him back his daughter.

Warden Hoffman stood behind his desk and stared out the window, overlooking the activists and TV crews gathering in the rain at his prison. Agent Lorenzo Callcut paced back and forth across the length of the room, clearly agitated.

"Warden, we need a total lockdown on Ramirez. If he knows we're involved then that girl is dead! We need more time." Callcut pleaded.

"He knows." Warden Hoffman said soberly.

Before Callcut could speak, there was a knock at the door. The door opened and a prison guard escorted Tony into the Warden's office.

"Sir, Mr. Evans as you requested." The guard turned and left the room, closing the door behind him.

"What do you mean he knows?" Callcut asked the Warden, ignoring Tony.

"He knows. His lawyers filed for a stay of execution with the Governor's office this morning. They're arguing that if Ramirez has any knowledge of the girl's kidnapping, then, the state can't carry out the execution—at least not until the girl is found."

"Ramirez isn't saying where his cousin is keeping Nicki. Is this what it's been about all along? All this talk about how he's ready to die was all bullshit. Ramirez is just looking for a way to get out of the needle. And let me guess, if the cops never find Nicki, then he lives his days out in prison or until his lawyer cuts a deal to get out in exchange for my daughter?" Tony asked.

"Cousin?" Callcut asked spinning around to face Tony.

"Yeah, Dante is Ramirez's cousin. They're family."

"Shit. Well, either way, that'll never happen. He ain't ever getting out."

"I agree, he'll never get out, but I can see them asking for a stay of execution until we find the girl. But if we never find the girl..." Warden Hoffman started to say.

"Then he never gets the needle. That's his motive for all this." Tony finished.

"Dante is not going to raise the kid. And they can't risk keeping her alive for such a desperate plan." offered Callcut.

"You think Dante will kill her, bury her someplace no one will ever find her, and tell the Governor that she is alive?" Tony asked, praying his theory was wrong.

Neither of the men looked at Tony nor said anything, leaving the question hanging in the air.

"The Governor can't give in. You think he will stay the execution?" Tony asked.

"He's a liberal. I really don't know. This has never happened to my knowledge. If he does, the risk is that every asshole on death row will make some play like this. That's the danger if he does give into Ramirez's lawyers." Warden Hoffman said.

"How did he know? How did Ramirez find out is what I want to know! Who has access to him?" Callcut asked.

"His lawyers, priest, and security detail. We held his mail. It's mostly fan mail anyway." Warden Hoffman said.

"Are you serious? Fan mail?" Tony asked, sickened.

"Killers, especially on death row, get a massive amount of mail. It's mostly from women. It's pretty sad if you ask me. I want two of my men to take one last shot at Ramirez." Callcut demanded of the Warden.

"The last interview didn't amount to anything?" Warden Hoffman asked.

"No, but I want them to go again with your permission of course."

"That's fine. I'll get him set up."

The three men stared out the windows, watching the TV and activist commotion below as the rain got heavier. Lost in their thoughts and the desperation of finding Nicki, no one said anything. Tony finally broke the silence.

"So, what do we do now?"

Chapter 22

"Will you look at this crap Mom?" Amy asked.

Amy, along with her mom and dad, gathered on a couch at the safe house to watch the TV news coverage of the top story of the day: the execution of Reynaldo Ramirez. Amy had been trying to ignore all the police protection assigned to her family by losing herself in the news. The last hour of coverage had been a methodical retracing of the life of Ramirez and his victims, both the people that he was convicted of murdering and the ones that he was suspected of killing. Interview after interview, rain poured down on sad women in raincoats and umbrellas, holding candles and begging for the Governor to spare Ramirez's life.

"An eye for an eye is not right. As a society, we have to forgive those that kill. If we kill people like Ramirez are we really any better than he is?" questioned a young woman being interviewed on TV, sucking up her fifteen minutes of fame.

"I bet she never had someone like Ramirez take *her* kid. Or kill someone in *her* family." Amy cried at the TV tearfully.

"Honey, we should just turn this off." Lindsay said, putting her arm around her daughter.

"I don't understand Mom. People like that woman! Is she actually crying for a murder? She wants to spare his life? Give him another chance? This idiot news lady is only presenting one side of the story. What about interviewing the family of the victims? Let's see how they feel about keeping this madman alive? I know that's not good TV. Where was this lady when some poor kid got a gun in his face? Who cries for those people?" Amy said growing more agitated.

"Honey, I know, I know. Please just calm down, Amy. It'll be all right." Lindsay comforted.

"This kind of coverage just sickens me. I think I'm gonna be sick!" Amy cried, ejecting herself off the couch and into the bathroom and slamming the door behind her.

"No news, Sir. Interview came up empty again." Officer Stevens reported, closing his phone and putting it back in his pocket. Callcut and Stevens rode up front, while Tony sat in the back of the police cruiser staring out the window at the cars passing by. Tony had his tattered backpack in his lap, headphones plugged into his tape recorder listening again to his last interview with Ramirez. Callcut headed south on the rain-slicked 580 towards highway 80 and then into San Francisco.

"Did Ramirez say anything useful?" Callcut asked Stevens.

"Guys said all he would talk about was his last murder: the one where he was picked-up. Something about, 'if anyone had any honor that would never have gone down,' whatever the hell that means."

"When he was arrested, and even in court, Ramirez claimed that he didn't kill anyone at the house. The police speculated that he knew one of the hookers, Julie Holloway. For some reason, Ramirez would never admit to why he'd gone there, but *something* happened that lead to the killings. During the trial the DA said that it was a jealousy thing with Ramirez and Julie and that Ramirez wanted her out of the business and went there to confront the pimp. Things got out of hand; Ramirez went on a rampage, then was shot during the exchange and captured. Everyone else died. That's the official story." Tony recounted.

"You don't believe that?" Callcut asked.

Tony turned off his tape recorder, pulled the headphones from his ears and leaned forward.

"Ramirez said he was there for Dante."

"Dante? What the hell are you talking about?"

"He said that he didn't know any 'Julie'. Maybe, maybe not. In my last interview with him, he said that Dante owed the pimp money and that he was being squeezed. He admitted to killing the pimp, but it was Dante that went ballistic and killed everyone. Sort of a 'getting rid of the witnesses' kind of a thing."

"Bullshit. I don't buy any of that. What evidence do we have that lends any weight to his story?" Callcut asked, looking at Tony in the review mirror.

"Ramirez said he was…wait hold on." Tony started to say as he reached into his backpack, and flipped through some folders and papers. Tony quickly pulled out a copy of the police report from the night Ramirez was arrested, opening the report and glancing at the photos taken at the crime scene.

"Ok, I didn't put this together before. The police recovered a .38 at the scene." Tony said.

"Yes, the pimp was killed with a .38, the women with a 9mm." Stevens recalled.

"The police assumed that the 9mm was Ramirez's, but *he* was shot with a 9mm. During the investigation the .38 was proven to be the pimp's, and there was no 9mm found at the scene. So, whose gun was it?" Tony asked.

"He got rid of it." Callcut dismissed.

"What if he didn't? Ramirez claims that Dante had the 9mm, went crazy and killed the witnesses, and Ramirez bounced because he knew that the cops would show up sooner or later, except he was shot in the leg and that slowed him down. Hear, listen to the tape."

Tony pulled the headphones out of the tape recorder, rewound the tape and played the last interview for them. When the interview was over, Tony turned off the tape and continued.

"What if the importance of this event is not the place, but the motive? Up to this point, Ramirez has wanted me to go to these places to find something. But this house was burned down in the nineties and replaced with several businesses over the years. There's a candle shop there now. The paper looked into it, and it checks out."

"So you're saying that Ramirez thinks that Dante shot him?" Callcut asked.

"Yeah, so Ramirez would get caught and be charged for the murders. What if Ramirez wanted to lead us to Dante as payback for putting him in prison? Remember, Ramirez is a dirt bag but has a strong since of honor. No matter how twisted it may seem, to him, blood is always thicker than water. His mother took the secret to her death bed, and Ramirez didn't sell out Dante during the trial. He took the heat for Dante, but Dante betrayed him by not owning up to his crime and laying low. Ramirez could have told us any bullshit story he wanted but he didn't. I believe he wants us to find Dante. With his statement on tape he could screw over Dante the same way he feels he got screwed over all those years ago." Tony stated, putting the theory together.

"Well, if that was the case then why not just tell us where Dante is?" Officer Stevens asked.

"Ramirez likes the game. He loves power. That's painfully obvious. In his head, he wins. Dante gets caught, he wins. He gets his life glamorized, he wins. He's responsible for Nicki's death, another murder to his name, and the cops fail, he wins. If the Governor stays his execution, he wins."

"If we go with that, then the sixty-four thousand dollar question is, 'Where the hell is Dante?'" Stevens asked.

"So, these interviews are all about the locations right?" Callcut asked Tony.

"Yeah, well, sort of. It seems that he's directing me to these places. He keeps going on about the ex-wife's place in Oakland, about which he clearly has a lot of anger. There's also the photo he wanted me to find of the warehouse that you raided. Dante was there. You have evidence of that."

"My money says Dante is hiding in that warehouse. Moving the kid around is too dangerous, and he may be thinking the last place we would look is the place we already raided."

"Callcut, his anger about his ex-wife is really strong. There's something about that crack house that bugs me."

Agent Callcut dismissed Tony's theory, "Too much activity to hide a kid. That would be too risky."

"Bobby and I were out there yesterday. It was dead man. I think..."

"It doesn't make sense Tony. Stevens, get a unit out to that warehouse, and get some eyes on it. Let's get someone out there to take a look." Callcut ordered.

"Callcut, I really think..." Tony started.

"Look that just doesn't make sense. When we get back, Stevens is staying with you. If we get anything on the warehouse, I'll let you know."

Tony leaned back against the seat, dejected by Callcut's stubbornness. The rest of the ride into San Francisco was quiet with the occasional blast of the police scanner breaking the silence.

"Look, this is bullshit Stevens and you know it!" Tony argued as he pulled the key out of his front door and entered his apartment followed by Stevens, who closed the door behind him.

"Look, it's for your own safety. We'll find her! Callcut's one of the best. We *will* find her."

"I can't just sit here. I can't just wait. I think we need to check out that drug den again. I'm telling you man, there's something there!"

"Tony. We need to wait...."

"Look, can we just get someone over there to watch the place? If he shows, then we would know, right?"

"We have eyes all over Dante's known stomping grounds. If he pops up, we'll get him."

"Please, Stevens, it's my kid. Do you have kids? What will it hurt?" Tony pleaded.

"I'll see what I can do." Stevens reluctantly pulled out his phone and started making calls.

Chapter 23

Night fell on San Francisco with a steady rain, but that didn't deter the activities and onlookers outside the San Quentin prison gates as people continued to gather for the candle light vigil for Reynaldo Ramirez. Light poles from the TV mobile crews illuminated reporters as they stared into the camera's eye, reporting the latest from the scene. Inside the prison walls, Reynaldo continued to be prepared for his death date with the state of California. During the afternoon, Reynaldo met with his priest and lawyer in the visiting room until about 6:15pm at which time the prison guards needed to take Ramirez for final processing. After his visitors left, Ramirez was taken to a holding cell behind the visitation room, strip-searched and given new prison issued clothes. After changing, Ramirez was handcuffed and escorted by six guards to the death chamber waiting room. The waiting room door was unlocked and Ramirez was moved inside and up against the far wall. A new group of prison guards, the Execution Squad, eight officers trained in the art of death for the state gathered around Ramirez. The lead guard, a six foot five, muscular man with a shave head, small glasses and a starched impeccable uniform faced Ramirez and stared into his eyes.

"Are we gonna have any problems when we take the cuffs off?"

Ramirez just shook his head no.

After the handcuffs were removed Ramirez was subject to yet another strip-search. Under the inspection of a flashlight, every orifice is searched and verified that there is no weapon or contraband hidden. The room temperature was very cold as Ramirez stood barefoot and defiant, refusing to give the guards the satisfaction of humiliation. When the guards were satisfied, Ramirez was given a new set of prison clothes. These would be the final set of clothes Reynaldo would ever wear. Ramirez was then cuffed and moved to new cell, just outside the death chamber doors. The cell was about half the size of his old cell, featuring only a toilet, mattress and pillow. The iron door was shut and bolted behind him. Un-cuffed Ramirez adjusted to his cramped surroundings. Shortly Reynaldo's priest and lawyer entered an adjoining holding cell, where they were allowed to speak and prey with Ramirez until it was time to be moved to the death chamber. At 7:30pm Ramirez silently ate his last meal of steak and potatoes. Slowly and methodically, he cut his food and watched the red juices flow and pool on the tin prison tray. He smiled at the irony as he savored every bite. Ramirez looked up periodically to watch prison officers pass by with armfuls of alcohol pads, swabs, and other equipment for his execution.

"What you got?" Callcut asked the officer as he slid into the passenger seat of the police cruiser to escape the rain.

"Yes Sir. I've been out here for a few hours. About thirty minutes ago, there was a light that went on inside the warehouse. It was on for a few minutes, and then went out. From here, I could see both Armstrong and Hawes Streets, and I didn't see anyone come or go. It may be nothing, but I was told to radio anything. I let my watch commander know. There!" The uniformed officer reported as he pointed to the light coming from the top floor of the Baxter and Son's warehouse.

As quickly as the light went on, the light went out again. Callcut pulled out his cell phone and speed dialed. Putting the phone to his ear, he waited for a response.

"Captain, it's Agent Callcut. We got something. Lights went on and off in the Baxter warehouse. We got some activity. It may be them. We need to roll."

"Screw this!" Tony launched himself from the couch, fed-up with waiting all day in his apartment with no news of his daughter from the police. "Am I under arrest?"

"No, of course not." replied Stevens as he came out of Tony's kitchen with a cup of coffee.

"And you have to go where I go right? Then get your jacket, I'm going to that fucking house to find my kid!" Tony grabbed his jacket, put it on and grabbed his wallet and keys off the kitchen table.

"I need to call it in."

"Do whatever you need to do. You're driving." Tony said, headed for the door.

Ramirez's priest read scripture from his Bible as his lawyer spoke quietly on his cell phone in the corner. Officer Samson and two other guards watched over Ramirez from the other side of the barred door. Samson looked at his watch and slowly approached the cage.

"One hour Ramirez."

"Any news?" Ramirez asked his lawyer, who looked back at the convicted killer and shook his head no.

Stevens and Tony pulled up and parked in front of the crack house off Martin Luther King Avenue. Stevens radioed in and shut off the engine. The two men stared through the pouring rain at the deserted-looking house. Tony was the first to reach for his door and get out of the car, followed by the police officer. The two men jogged across the street to the opening in the fence. Tony led the way into the empty lot, trying to ignore the pouring rain. The abandoned cars were still lined up, yet there was no one around.

"Don't you think it's odd that there's not a single junkie around?" Tony whispered.

Stevens ignored Tony and moved out front, taking point. He made his way around to the back of the building, reached down and unsnapped the holster on his belt, but didn't remove his service weapon.

"All units are in place, Sir." said a uniformed officer perched by Callcut's window.

"Thanks." Switching on his radio, Callcut told all units to be at the ready.

Ramirez stood up, staring blankly at the priest, Warden, Samson, and the Execution Squad who gathered on the other side of the iron bars. Ramirez knew this was his last walk down these halls, yet he showed no emotion to anyone standing before him. Samson stepped to the front of the cage.

"Turn around, on your knees, hands on your head, fingers locked. You know the drill. One last time for us."

Chapter 24

Officer Stevens tried the back door only to find it locked. Using a tactical flashlight, he looked over the condition of the door and the door frame. After sizing it up, he drew his service weapon and kicked in the door. The door broke away from the lock and swung open. Tony was hit by the stale, nasty air he remembered from earlier in the week. That odor in cold, wet air was no improvement. Holding back the urge to retch, Tony paused behind Stevens in the hallway.

"You want to wait outside?" Officer Stevens whispered.

Tony shook his head and pointed up the stairs. Pulling his jacket over his nose and mouth, he willed his body to move forward deeper into the stench and darkness.

Ramirez lay on his back, staring up at the blank prison execution room ceiling. He rolled his head to look out through the large window that separated the gallery from the prisoner. Officers of the death squad strapped his legs and arms down. As Ramirez scanned the audience who had gathered to watch his death, the only familiar face he knew was his court-appointed lawyer. When the last restraint on his arm was cinched down, a doctor came to his side and rubbed an alcohol swab on his arm. Ramirez laughed out loud at the irony of making sure he didn't get an infection from a needle designed to kill him. Surprised at the laughter, the doctor stepped away from Ramirez. After a moment, the doctor regained his composure and returned to his duties. He placed the needle in Ramirez's arm and checked the tubing that ran to the electronic device that would administer the deadly cocktail to Ramirez's body. Once started, the device couldn't be stopped. When the doctor had completed his review, he nodded to the Warden, who nodded back. Ramirez and the Warden looked up at the clock, noting the time: 11:55pm. Ramirez looked over at the priest, who had his head down and was clutching his Bible to his chest, praying silently. The priest raised his eyes to meet those of Ramirez, and then looked away.

Callcut and his team worked their way to the breach points of the Baxter and Son's warehouse. With SWAT and SFPD officers in place, Callcut gave the order to go. Police breached the outer doors and stormed the warehouse for a second time that week. Callcut and team breached the front door and swept the bottom floor without incident. Rushing the stairwell to the upper floor, their searchlights shone on every corner. Two homeless people cowered in the far corner of the warehouse. A man struggled to pull his pants up as a woman scampered in the shadows behind him, trying to pull her dirty and torn shirt down over her head with one hand and her sweat pants up with the other. Finally the man got his pants in place as the woman ducked behind him, trying to finish dressing.

"What the hell???" sputtered the homeless man.

"Police! Stay right there! Don't move!" ordered the officer, shining his light at the pair.

The overhead lights sprang to life as Agent Callcut walked up behind the officer, putting his hand on the officer's weapon, and lowering the light beam to the floor.

"Are you the only ones here?" the agent asked.

"Yeah, Jesus, man! Talk about a cock block. You really know how to ruin a moment!"

"Yeah, sorry about that. Did you see anyone else here? How long have you been here?"

"No, no one. That's why we came here. We haven't been here that long."

"No one with a kid? A girl?"

"No. No one."

"The lights? Was that you guys?"

"Yes! Do you mind? Can I get dressed?" The woman begged from behind the man, still struggling to get her shirt over her head.

Callcut shook his head, smiling at her fury, and turned to the officers behind him. "Call it in and kick 'em loose."

The clock read 11:58pm. While all eyes were on the clock, and the doctor stood at the ready, the real attention was focused on the wall phone just next to the Warden. Ramirez looked over at the priest who shook his head ever so slightly. Ramirez knew that the only thing that would keep him alive was a call from the Governor. As the minute hand continued to tick towards the zero hour, beads of sweat formed on Ramirez's forehead, and he silently counted every shallow breath he took.

Stevens moved his way slowly down the dark hallway of the crack house. Tony pointed to the last door on the left as they worked their way towards the end of the hall. Stevens did a quick sweep of each room he came across, each one as vacant as the previous one. When they reached the last doorway, Stevens swung around into the room, scanning from one side to the other with the flashlight, revealing nothing. Empty. Tony noted that the dead body that was there a few days ago had been removed, but nothing else was different.

"No! NICKI!" Tony screamed out as Stevens dropped his weapon to his side and listened to the name echo though the house. A muffled sound followed by a thumping noise emanated from the other end of the hallway. In unison, the men rushed out of the room and headed towards the sound.

"Nicki!" Tony called out again.

The banging renewed like someone kicking a wall. The pouring rain dripping through holes in the ceiling garbled the sound, but as the two men made their way down the stairs, a loud crash on the wood floor erupted from where they'd entered the building.

"What the fuck is this bullshit!" Dante yelled, as he dropped two plastic bags of groceries.

Stevens quickly snapped off his light and motioned for Tony to freeze. The muffled sound renewed, catching everyone's attention, especially Dante's.

"Shut the hell up!" Dante said as he walked through the darkness towards the back of the kitchen. Kneeling down, he put a key in a padlock and removed the lock to a cellar door.

"And for you dust heads that broke my fucking door! You better be gone after I deal with this bitch!"

"NICKI!" Tony screamed, unable to control himself.

"POLICE! FREEZE!" Stevens ordered.

Dante spun around without looking and rapidly fired three shots into the darkness of the hallway. Tony dove around the banister as wood splintered into the air from one of the bullet impacts. Stevens gasped as he fired off two rounds. Dante shouted out, and there was a loud thud in the darkness of the kitchen. Stevens coughed and struggled to rise to his knees.

"Stevens! Are you alright? Where you hit? I think you got him!" Tony said from behind the banister, trying to scan the darkness for signs of Dante.

Stevens shone his light down the hallway towards the kitchen. He lit up Dante, standing right in front of him with his left arm hanging down at his side pouring blood on the floor, and his right hand pointing his pistol at Stevens. The light startled Dante, momentarily preventing him from firing the fatal shot. Tony, without thinking, rushed Dante, laying into his midsection and tackling him to the ground, sending the pistol flying into the air and into the darkness beyond them.

Tony quickly jumped on top of Dante, punching with everything he had towards Dante's face. Dante blocked many of the shots with his right but had trouble lifting his left. Dante grabbed Tony by the throat, pulled him closer to his face, getting Tony's weight off his hips, and was able to buck him off of him. Tony, caught by surprise, sprawled across the floor face down. Before he got up, he felt Dante's boot in his side, kicking the air out of his lungs. With Tony gasping for breath, Dante kicked him repeatedly in the ribs. Tony balled up, trying to protect himself.

"You motherfucker! I should have aced your ass back at your friend's place! I'll take care of that right now, then that bitch of yours!" Dante screamed at Tony.

Reaching into his back pocket, Dante pulled out a knife, swiping the blade into the locked position. Tony put his hands in a defensive position trying to protect his face staying balled up into the fetal position.

"Ramirez KNOWS!" Tony blurted out in desperation.

"What are you talking about, dead man? He knows what?" Dante asked, delaying his assault.

"He knows you set him up!"

"Set him up? I didn't set anyone up."

"You shot him! Years ago! In Oakland! He knows you shot him to take the rap for your murders!"

"I didn't shoot my cousin. One of them bitches tried to take my gun and it went off. I got it back and killed her just like I'm going to kill you!"

"Think about it, how do you think we found you here? Ramirez wanted us to find you here! He knew this is where you would have my daughter. He sent us to find you."

"My cousin would never fuck me over like that! We have each other's back!" Dante yelled at Tony.

"Then why are we HERE? Think about it!" Tony demanded, trying to move slowly away from Dante.

Dropping to one knee over Tony, he lifted the blade high into the air and paused. Tony could see deep into Dante's eyes as the flicker of doubt ignited. Dante reached back into his memories and started to connect the dots and couldn't understand why his cousin would set him up. He had done everything that Ramirez asked of him, all the way to the smallest detail. Going back to the night of Ramirez's capture Dante thought, *"Why would his cousin not rat him out to the cops? It was out of family loyalty, right? Family doesn't screw each other over. Reynaldo couldn't possibly think that he would really shoot him, would he?"* Then it hit Dante, *"Revenge is a dish best served cold."*

"That son of a bitch!" Dante yelled as he reached the most logical conclusion and realized that Tony was right. This was a set-up from the beginning.

"NO!" Tony yelled as he tried to squirm away from Dante as Dante's attention was now squarely directed at Tony.

Dante lunged forward and started to thrust the knife viciously downwards towards Tony when a gunshot rang out, shattering the stale air, followed closely by two more shots. Dante fell across Tony's curled-up body and refused to move. Tony could feel the warm, sticky blood flow across his skin.

Tony kicked Dante off him and stood up. Stevens shone his light on Tony and the dead body of Dante, three bullet holes in his back, blood reflecting off the light. Neither man spoke. The sound of rain pounding against the roof was deafening to Tony.

"Go." Stevens urged.

Tony grabbed the flashlight that Stevens extended towards him and raced to the kitchen. He swung open the heavy wooden door and shined the light down the stairs into the darkness.

"Nicki?" Tony shouted.

A muffled sound came from the emptiness. Tony descended the stairs and shone the light around the cellar. It was damp and musty, polluted with garbage. Nicki lay on her side, tied to an armless kitchen chair. She had worked the rope on her left leg loose enough that she could kick the wall with just enough force to get her father's attention. Her eyes widened in the light like a trapped wild animal.

"Oh my God! Nicki! Stevens, she's here!" Tony called out.

Tony ran over to his daughter, jamming the light into his mouth to help him see what he was doing, and untied her as fast as he could. Beaten, bloodied, and bruised, she cried at the sight of her father. He freed her from her bindings and pulled the gag from her mouth. She kicked the chair away and lunged into the father's arms. Tony held Nicki with all his might, never wanting to let her go. He picked her up and carried her up the stairs. They found Stevens in the kitchen, removing his Kevlar vest and examining the wound on his left bicep. Looking up at Tony with his daughter in his arms, he smiled at the two of them.

"Damn, that hurts. Hi, sweetie. I'm Stevens. Sorry we took so long."

Ramirez watched the minute hand click up towards midnight. The priest slowly walked across the room towards Ramirez, head down, Bible to his chest. Ramirez looked up to the priest as he leaned over Ramirez's head. Ramirez could see the small wire coming under the priest's collar and into his ear. The priest leaned close to Ramirez's ear and whispered to him.

"Just came over the police scanner, it's done. Your cousin is dead. Go with God my son."

The priest slowly backed away from the prisoner and resumed his place in the death chamber. Ramirez smiled to himself, satisfied that he had achieved his final killing. He was now at peace and ready to die.

When the minute hand struck the zero hour, he flashed one last look towards the phone for a call that would never come. The Warden nodded to the doctor, who then switched on the device. A low hum filled the air. A snap of the first button sent the first of three plungers down, pumping the fluid into Ramirez's arm. Ramirez closed his eyes and smiled, entertained by his own thoughts. By the time the second plunger finished delivering its payload, Ramirez's body had gone rigid and had started to convulse. By the time the third plunger emptied, Ramirez lay still on the table. The doctor moved over the hulking silent body, and used his stethoscope to listen for a pulse. After a quick examination, he looked to the Warden and nodded.

"Time of death, five minutes past midnight. This concludes the execution of Reynaldo Ramirez." Warden Hoffman announced to the gallery as the curtains closed in the observation window.

Chapter 25

Late Sunday morning in room 221 at San Francisco General Hospital and Trauma Center, Nicki Evans sat upright in her hospital bed. Even with tubes in her arms and nurses fussing over her, she was in great spirits, happy to be reunited with her parents. Surrounded by flowers, balloons, and teddy bears from family, the San Francisco Police Department, the Chronicle newspaper staffers, the hospital, TV news stations, and the public, Nicki felt overwhelmed. Gathered up in her mother's arms, she listed as the news report boomed from the TV mounted in the corner of the room. At the bottom of the screen she could see CNN's breaking news: *missing 11-year-old girl found safe in daring rescue by her father and police in San Francisco.*

The story had gone nationwide. Finally a feel good story for America's public. It wasn't often that a kidnapped victim was found alive and well.

Agent Callcut came into the room, his arms filled with more balloons and a teddy bear for Nicki. He took the large bear to Nicki then placed the rest of the balloons down in the corner of the hospital room. Amy slid off the bed and wrapped her arms around the officer. Callcut then went over to Tony who had been sitting on a padded bench next to the hospital window. Tony had been reading the morning edition of the San Francisco Chronicle and the lead story about the death of Bobby Jenkins. It was a fitting piece written by Carol Gibson. Tony knew he owed her a debt that he might never be able to repay. He dropped the paper down on the couch and slowly stood up, holding his ribs.

"Tony, how are you holding up? Doc said you'd be OK." Agent Callcut said smiling warmly at Tony.

"I'll live. Two cracked ribs, but nothing too bad. Looks like it might take a little time, but Nicki's going to be fine. The doctors said that the physical wounds will heal, but they're more concerned about the psychological damage though. I guess it's just going to take some time."

"She wasn't... I mean you know—he didn't abuse her any other way did he?" Callcut asked quietly.

"No, thank God."

"Great. That's great news to hear. You never know about these twisted..." Callcut stopped himself, remembering Nicki's presence.

"I know. No, I know she is going to be fine. How's Stevens?" Tony asked, changing the subject.

"He took two rounds to the chest and one in the arm. That Kevlar saved his life, but I can tell you from experience that it still hurts like a bitch. He's upstairs in 369—you should go and see him. He had surgery last night on the arm, but he should be up and around soon. Hey, listen, man—I'm sorry I didn't listen to you. That could have been a fatal mistake, and I'm sorry."

"Callcut, its fine. No harm, no foul. We got her. She's safe and that's all that matters right? She's alive and the bad guys all died." Tony extended his hand to the FBI agent.

"Yeah, no harm, no foul. So all of this was for Ramirez to get revenge on his cousin?"

"Yeah, Ramirez thought Dante shot him to take the rap but it turns out though that Dante didn't shoot Ramirez. One of the working girls fought for Dante's gun and it went off, hitting Ramirez. It looks like Ramirez setup his cousin over an accident and bad assumption."

"Sucks to be Dante, doesn't it?" Callcut said, smiling at Tony.

"Daddy, come sit with me!" Nicki said, breaking into their conversation.

"And with that, I will get out of here. Take care of yourself Tony. Go take care of your family."

"That I will. Thanks again for everything."

Tony shook his hand again and smiled as the agent left the room, and then joined his wife and daughter on the hospital bed. Holding Nicki's hand and wrapping an arm around Amy, Tony made a silent commitment to take Callcut's advice, "I AM going to take care of my family!" With renewed conviction, he embraced the two most important people in his life. He never wanted to let go of either ever again.

Chapter 26: Epilogue

The Barnes and Noble bookstore on 82nd and Broadway in New York's Upper West Side near Central Park was bustling with people in anticipation of the book by new author Tony Evans. The media blitz started months before with Tony making the rounds on all the talk and news shows to promote his new book *The Zero Hour*. It had been a tough but successful year for the Evans. Tony began writing his book almost immediately and with the advances from the book publisher was able to get counseling for Nicki and his wife. The first few months Tony and Nicki were local celebrities doing TV and radio interviews. As time passed life slowed down as Tony focused on his relationship with his family and writing his book. Nicki had a hard time for months, waking up in the middle of the night to face her nightmares. Time heals all wounds and Nicki's wounds slowly healed also. Now with the book finally out, Tony was making appearances with his family as they told their story over and over for all of America to hear. The public couldn't seem to get enough of their story, and it was reflected in the pre-orders of the book. As midnight in New York approached, people lined up all through the store and outside, braving the light snow on a cold November night for their chance to meet the man who saved his daughter from evil and rediscovered family bliss.

"Tony! I've got great news! I just got word that Zero Hour will hit the best sellers list!" Tony's agent and publicist Bernard Cummings announced with the enthusiasm of a teenage girl seeing a pop star for the first time. Bernard may have been only five-foot-six, flamboyantly gay, and dressed in suits that were over-the-top for Tony's taste, but he couldn't deny Bernard's passion for his work.

"That's great, Bernard. That's just fantastic!" Tony said as he entered the store, waving to waiting customers. Bernard moved ahead of Tony and ensured that the table was stocked with plenty of pens and a pitcher of water with a plastic cup. Tony took his seat at the table and looked over the crowd in disbelief that all these people were really here to see him and buy his book. He smiled and nodded at Bernard to invite the customers to meet the newest and hottest author on the New York Bestseller's list.

"I am so happy to meet you, Mr. Evans. I've followed your story, and I can't imagine what happened to your family happing to mine. Your story is truly inspiring." gushed the first customer in line, a very pretty single mom with her teenage son by her side, grinning from ear to ear.

"That's very kind. Who do I make this out to?"

The evening stretched into the early morning hours as Tony worked through his long line of fans. As the event wound down Tony signed the last books for the remaining few customers that braved the cold on his behalf. Tony looked up and smiled at his beautiful wife and daughter who were standing near the employee entrance in the back of the store, waiting for him. New York had always held a special place for Tony as this was where he first met Amy, and though he didn't know it at the time, it was the real start of his life. After the last book was signed, Tony stacked the remaining books and joined his wife.

Tony took Amy's hands, kissed her deeply on the lips, and embraced her tightly. She wrapped her arms around his waist and buried her face into his chest.

"I love you honey." Tony said to Amy.

"I love you too baby."

Nicki came up behind her mom and threw her arms around her parents and held them tight too. Tony and Amy laughed at her and held her close between them.

"Yes, Nicki, we love you too!" Tony and Amy said, laughing.